Bravery comes in all shapes and forms. Even when there was no hope left, you made me laugh and forget.

We will always have our final stroll through the orchard.

Tough times don't last. Tough people do.

This one's for you Dad x

PROLOGUE
BLAKE

She was so fucking gorgeous, it hurt. I took her mouth to mine and devoured her smooth lips. Her hands clawed around my neck, and mine circled her waist, pulling her closer in my lap. All the noise, music, and party swirling around us disappeared when our tongues assaulted one another in a heated kiss.

"Get a room." A voice echoed over the thudding bass. Lily smiled against my lips, and damn, this girl was the stars.

I pulled away breathlessly, and half-hooded eyes stared back at me. We were at my friend, Fabian's oceanfront mansion. I'd graduated high school today and was hours into the after-party celebrating with my girl and now-drunk school friends.

Glass bottles lay strewn across marble tabletops and ashtrays overflowed with burned-out cigarettes. The music blared out of the stereo speakers, and the living room was alive with bodies—mostly inebriated, drunk-ass bodies grinding on each other.

Dressed in a strapless canary-yellow dress that matched her

1

blonde hair and smoky popping blue eyes, my heart leaped into my chest when she arrived on my doorstep.

And now, the more our tongues entangled, the more obvious the bulge in my pants. But we hadn't gone all the way yet, and as much as I wanted my best friend, I didn't push. Watching her come when I was between her legs was enough for now.

She lowered her mouth to my ear, her warm breath falling on my cheek. "Can we go somewhere?" she asked as her chest rose and fell quickly against my own.

"You read my mind," I added, trailing her jaw and grazing her skin with delicate licks and bites. She moaned in my ear, and the sound made my dick swell. My hands circled her hips, and I lifted her off my lap, setting her upright.

We walked hand in hand through the drunk haze of my school friends. Then I started taking the steps two at a time. She kept up, desperate like me to be alone.

I opened the door to Fabian's room. The high bright moon turned the dark room into gray.

Lily sat on the bed, crossing her legs, and gestured for me to sit beside her.

"This is nice," she said with a satisfied smile.

"You're nice." I walked over and leaned down, pressing my lips to hers.

Our kiss turned heated in a millisecond. Lily's breath was ragged like mine, her skin hot to the touch. Fuck, it took everything inside me to take a physical step back before I lost all control and tore off her damn dress.

She held her arm out, wanting me to come back. "Blake, I'm ready."

I blinked, unsure I heard her correctly.

As if sensing my hesitation, she spoke again. "I want to take the next step with you."

I raked a hand through my hair, not moving my balled fist

from the crown of my head. Never once in the last few months had anything felt forced or contrived, and we'd done everything else imaginable. The last thing I wanted was for her to feel pressured now. "Are you sure?"

She gazed up at me with innocent blue eyes and dragged her teeth across her bottom lip. "I trust you, Blake."

Without waiting for me to reply, she stood and turned round, inviting me to unzip her dress. I stepped closer, all my nerves firing with the realization this was actually happening.

I glided the zipper down and slid it over her hips, revealing her black thong and the bare, beautiful curves of her back.

My hand circled her hip, spinning her around to face me. I drew in a sharp breath. "Fuck, you're beautiful."

She smiled slightly, but I could tell she was nervous.

I pulled her close, palming her other hip, closing the gap between us. "If, at any moment, you don't want this, Lily, just say so."

She nodded. "Okay."

I swallowed down the lump in my throat, steering away sudden nerves.

When the fuck did I get nervous?

I wanted this to be perfect.

Sliding one finger between her skin and the fabric lace of her thong, I glided it down past her thighs to the floor. She stepped out of it, and I dropped to my knees. Damn, I couldn't wait any longer to taste her.

"Blake, I said I'm ready."

"Don't deprive me, baby." Then, without waiting for her to reply, I swiped my tongue over her clit, and she released an audible gasp.

My dick ached, swelling to a dangerous size as it strained against my zipper.

I buried my face deeper, and she gripped the back of my hair between her fingertips and groaned loudly.

"Shh, baby," I leaned back and whispered.

She was close. So close. From a bended knee, I greedily swiped her sex, dragging her wetness up to her clit with long, punishing strokes until she saw stars.

"What was that?" she asked. Her hands fell from my head and cradled my face as she looked down at me in awe.

I let out a throaty groan and licked her orgasm off my lips, savoring her sweetness. "I just want to make sure you really want this."

She let out a laugh. "Well, if you wanted me to change my mind, you shouldn't have made me come!" A grin spread on her lips as she dragged me up by the shirt and unbuttoned it. "Because I want to come all over again."

She took her lips to mine, our breathing irregular from the desire flooding our bones.

"Damn, I like the sound of that." I legged out of my suit pants and boxers and jerked out of my shirt. Lily lay back on the bed, her eyes dragging up and down my body. Never, ever, did I think this day would come.

The girl next door, my best friend, lay splayed out in front of me, wanting me.

Taking a condom from my wallet, I stepped back toward the foot of the bed, scouring her face for approval. She dragged her eyes up from my hard dick and, without hesitation, nodded for me to continue.

My eyes went wide at the realization. Lily wanted me to be her first. God knows why. She could have anyone, but she trusted *me*.

Quickly, I rolled on the condom and climbed over her, ensuring my weight was displaced, resting my elbows on either side of her head.

"Kiss me," she breathed out, biting down on her lip.

I pushed away a wayward blonde hair on her cheek and dragged my lips across hers, wanting to take away her nervousness. Then I trailed her neck with kisses, arriving at her smatter of freckles along her collarbone. She tilted her head back, and at the same time, her legs parted beneath me. The tip of my dick dipped along her warm, moist folds then I pressed against her sex.

Her hands circled my waist and pulled me down to her, so our bodies touched. My chest pressed into her soft tits. Warm and smooth, her body felt like home. Slowly, I guided my cock inside her wet folds, and her nails dug deep into my back, followed by a sharp inhale.

I froze, scared I'd hurt her. "You okay?" I whispered into the shell of her ear.

"I'm fine. Please don't stop."

She dragged my mouth to hers, kissing me between short, ragged breaths. I moved again, my dick nudging the rest of the way inside her slippery entrance.

"Fuck," I bit out at the overwhelming sensation.

She was tight and perfect, and my eyes rolled in the back of my head.

Slowly, I started rolling my hips, sliding in and out of her. Then I felt her grip loosen, and my pace quickened. Her moans grew louder as she pulled herself onto me. Unable to contain myself, I thrust into her harder and felt her clench around my cock.

"Blake," she breathed out in a moan before finding her release. I couldn't hold it any longer. With my body pressed against hers, I came in an explosion of desire.

When I opened my eyes, she was staring straight at me, and something inside me suddenly shifted. I was free-falling without a net, and a heavy ache settled in the center of my chest.

This was too much.

1

LILY

SIX YEARS LATER

U nable to withstand being there anymore, I snuck out of the karaoke club.

My two besties, Jazzie and Amber, belted out rather boisterously, "YMCA" while I slipped through the exit door. They were not alone. They had the golden tones of Kit Jones, an international rock star from the band, Four Fingers, and Jazzie's boyfriend.

I glanced over my shoulder as I exited the building. As grateful as I was that Kit flew us over to see Jazzie, watching them together twisted my stomach into a ball of knots. Don't get me wrong, I was truly happy for Jazzie, but the chemistry that passed between them was a stark reminder of my past.

Once upon a time, I was the most important person to Blake Carter.

Until he took my precious V-card and left without so much as a goodbye.

The chill in the night sky hit me like a slap to the face. I pulled my mauve coat tighter around my waist and hailed a cab with my free hand. *Shit. Was I really doing this?*

"Where to?" The middle-aged man's accent was thick, his smile unusually warm.

"Corner of Lexington and East 65th Street, please." The address burned a hole in my pocket, but I needn't look at the crumpled piece of paper that hid there.

Before leaving Australia for New York, Blake's Dad, Alistair, had scribbled down his son's address. It was tempting to let it sit and gather a film of dust like the yellow pages stacked next to it. *But I couldn't do it.* I'd memorized the address before the ink had even dried. As much as Blake had ruined me, he'd saved me too, and I just couldn't ignore that. Then there was the fact Alistair hadn't seen his son in six years, and I scored a free flight. I promised him I'd visit Blake for both of us.

The cab sped off toward the address, and I settled into my seat. Nerves stretched across my rib cage, settling in the base of my belly. I took a deep breath to steady myself, but its effect was fleeting.

Blake and Alistair were the family I never had. The three of us jelled from the very beginning. Nothing was ever forced or contrived, uncomfortable, or fake, unlike my aunt, who became my legal guardian at the tender age of fifteen.

The day I arrived in small-town Seaview, I ran straight out of my aunt's house into the back garden, wishing I'd wake up from the nightmare. Grief-stricken and broken, I'd lost my parents to a car accident days earlier. I hid in the overgrown backyard where my aunt couldn't find me, tears burning down my cheeks. Both anger and sadness coursed through my veins. At that moment, starting a new school and living a life without my parents was just unfathomable.

So when a basketball landed over the fence—just missing my head—the distraction pulled me out of my downward spiral, and I immediately threw it back. Like a bullet, all my anger and confusion welded into that single pass.

"That's some arm you got there," a voice sounded beyond the fence.

That's when I met him. Blake. The neighbor with sandy-brown hair and a cut-off tank top propped his head above the fence, his green eyes shining in the midday sun.

He was all smiles and warmth. Everything I craved. Waving me over, he hadn't noticed my red-tinged eyes. "You must be the new neighbor. With that arm, you ought to come over and shoot some hoops with my old man and me."

Meeting Blake Carter churned the contents of my stomach and made me forget about being alone. So naturally, outside of school, I spent every waking moment with him.

He wasn't like the other boys I knew. I was fifteen, and he was sixteen. Taller than me and lean with muscles, his hair feathered across his vibrant emerald greens.

Over time, my daily visits through the wonky fence pickets grew into something else. I wouldn't leave the house without some gel through my blonde hair and a dash of blue eyeliner to match my baby blues. A blot off some lip gloss, and I was ready. Then my outfits changed. Short shorts instead of baggy pants to show off my legs or a tank top to show my midriff.

He'd seek ways to touch me more. A slight finger grazed or a hand fell around my hips when we played ball. Then playing ball turned into hanging out in his tree house. Fast forward to his graduation dinner, followed by the after-party at an ocean-front mansion. He took my V-card in his best friend's bedroom.

And never looked back.

The cab pulled to an abrupt halt. "We're here," the driver announced.

Pulling my coat tighter around my waist, I glanced out the triangle window, where little veined icicles sprouted on the glass. My warm breath fogged the window as the cab sat idling on the Upper East Side.

"That will be eleven twenty."

9

My heart thudded. *Fuck, I was actually here. What now?*

The man cleared his throat, causing me to divert my attention to him. He scratched his beard, his worn eyes growing more impatient by the second.

"Sorry." Unzipping my crossbody bag, I pulled out my purse, noticing the tremble spreading up from my hands.

"Where in Aussie are you from?"

"A town called Seaview. You probably never heard of it." He shook his head. "It's a small coastal town in Queensland."

"Queensland? It's hot there, right? Beats the hell out of our winters."

"I don't know how you stand it. The cold, that is… my face feels like it's going to fall off." Trying to find American coins mixed with my Aussie money wasn't easy.

Oblivious to my struggle, he laughed. "You get used to it. Spring has sprung, so it's milder now."

After three merlots, digging for dimes and nickels with a shaking hand wasn't happening. "Here." I pulled a bill from my purse and thrust it toward him.

"Thanks, mate!" He tossed me a wayward wink. It was the worst attempt at an Aussie accent I'd ever heard.

I laughed, welcoming the distraction. "Oh please, don't ever do that again!"

He chuckled, then fiddled with his next booking on the screen.

I stared at the front door of the apartment building. Ornate lighting lit up the white block façade. Umbrellaed by a massive awning, the main steel door and black arched windows framed the grand entrance. Crisscrossed with black metal, they led to a foyer with a chandelier too ostentatious to put into words.

My heart thundered. Blake lived *here?*

Now what? I hadn't actually thought it through.

Would I just buzz his apartment? It was after eleven at

night. Would he even be home? It was Saturday night in bustling Manhattan.

"Are you getting out now?" Ahmed, according to the name on his cab ID, shifted in his driver's seat.

Dammit. I hadn't seen him in six years. I'd probably never see him again. There was no way I could afford a ticket to New York.

"Yes, I should go, shouldn't I?" I chewed the edge of my nail, twisting it between my teeth.

Ahmed's eyes flashed with confusion.

Fuck. He must think I'm strange. *I swear not all Australians are this odd.*

Car lights streamed through the windshield, and I put my hand up to my eyes, shielding the flow of high beams temporarily blinding me.

"Come on, turn off your high beams!" Ahmed yelled out the window, but the car couldn't hear from that far away. "You all right, sugar?"

I wasn't sure if he was referring to my temporary blindness or because my ass was glued to the seat.

"You certainly don't fit the criteria of New York cabbies, Ahmed."

I was stalling, but whatever.

"The criteria?"

"You obviously haven't read the Lonely Planet's guide to Manhattan. Crazy drivers, rude as hell, and moody. You know?"

He bellowed with laughter. "Well, I was born in Cairo. I've been a cabbie here for two years. Give it time." He turned toward the glaring lights. "Actually, this idiot is bothering me. Watch this." He cracked open the window and stuck his head out. "Hey, you're blinding us over here," he yelled to the cab driver opposite.

"Fuck off," a voice from outside yelled back. The driver

opposite pulled out, his high beams no longer streaming in and blinding Ahmed and me.

"Well, there you have it. A bit of New York, tailor-made just for you."

I giggled. "Thanks."

He regarded me, and I realized I still hadn't moved from my seat. *Well, it's now or never.* I let out a sigh, then pulled my bag to my chest. A man and woman walked past and toward the double doors. Her hand fell into his trench. The scantly-clad woman draped across him, unsteady on her feet and clawed at his neck.

Under the glow of the foyer lights, she pushed him against the wall, shoving her tongue down his throat in an over-the-top drunken kiss.

"Get a room," Ahmed yelled, thinking the same thing as me. "I could get used to this!"

Fuck's sake, what have I started?

The well-dressed man pulled back from sucking off the woman's face. Dressed in a woolen trench, scarf, and pointy shoes, he stepped closer toward us. I froze. The same cut of his jaw, full lips, and almond-shaped eyes that graced my dreams stared back at me.

Blake. My stomach flipped into two as emotion clogged my throat.

I leaned back, pushing as far back into my seat as I could, trying to hide in the shadows. I wanted the seat to dissolve and swallow me completely.

"Ahmed, drive," I whispered.

He turned round. "What's that?"

"Go, just go. *Drive!*"

Blake stared back at me into the dark cab. Quickly, I turned and stapled the back of my head to the seat, staring dead ahead. Ahmed turned around, his face etched with confusion.

"Mind your own business," a voice echoed down the half-empty street, his tone dark and more gravelly than I remembered but clearly Blake's.

"Ahmed, go now." My voice shook with fear as my throat closed up.

Ahmed pressed the accelerator, and the car lurched forward a few seconds after. Only then did the breath I was holding finally escape.

Tears pricked the backs of my eyes, but there was no way I'd let them spill over. I'd cried too many tears over Blake Carter.

That chapter in my life was shut, never *ever* to be reopened.

2

LILY

ONE MONTH LATER

listair was literally knee-deep in the veggie patch, harvesting the last of the tomatoes when I glanced over the fence. The owners of the house where I lived with my aunt had just completed a new wrap-around deck, and it was stunning.

I slumped my shoulders. *Aunt Josie.*

I'd promised to visit her when she moved but hadn't. It was one of those promises I hadn't really intended on keeping— half-hearted at best—and she knew that. It wasn't like my phone was ringing off the hook, so I thought I was in the clear.

She did the best she could. We both did, under the circumstances. I didn't blame her. Inheriting a fifteen-year-old when she'd just turned fifty, who'd want that? I was grateful she took me in, especially since she and Dad were estranged. But I was a minor with nowhere else to go. I barely knew who she was when I was thrust onto her doorstep, but we made it work for the three years we spent together.

As soon as my eighteenth birthday rolled around, Aunt Josie declared she needed more excitement in her life, sold the house, and moved out of small-town Seaview to the city. It wasn't too difficult to say goodbye and hardly sentimental. I'd spent more time with Blake and Al next door than I had with her. So when she sold and I was scouting for places to rent, Al asked me to move into the garden cottage he and Blake built at the rear of the property.

Al was my surrogate dad, and he meant the world to me. He'd already been on his own for a year after Blake left, so when he offered me the garden cottage at a modest rent, it was a no-brainer, and naturally, I had jumped at the chance.

Deep down, I think Alistair knew what happened with his son and me, although I never shared it. In the days that followed when Blake left, Al was there for me. When I should have been comforting him, he caught my tears and was the crutch I desperately needed.

He could have easily earned double the amount of rent had he tried. Still nursing my broken heart with little money to my name, it was easy to take him up on the offer. And I helped to maintain the enormous property, especially as he wasn't getting any younger.

The timing had been perfect, and we have coexisted ever since. Al lived in the main house with me in the cottage at the back. We spent loads of time together, working on the veggie patch and orchard that spawned between the houses.

"Lily, would you give me a hand with this?" Al asked, wiping the sweat from his brow.

I set my cup of peppermint tea down on the rusty table for two, ready to get my hands dirty.

"Don't get old, Lil. My hands are like stiff rods."

"Here, let me." I bent down and, with two hands, yanked the stubborn weed out from its roots.

"Don't go dirtying yourself now."

"Since when have I ever worried about that, Al?" I scoffed.

He smiled. Deep lines carved across his forehead like wood, and the wrinkles in the corners of his eyes and mouth told the story of a man who had dedicated his life to bettering that of his only son. I wondered what time he started this morning to already look so fatigued.

"This is a big job." He star-fished his stiff fingers to try and breathe some life back into them.

Al had the same eyes and tall build as his son. The difference was Al's heart was pure.

"I'd love to help you. You know that."

He winked. "I do. But now, look at you. All pretty as a peach in your flowery dress."

"Well, I am going to my floristry class." I smiled, pumped for today's class.

"At the community college? How's it going?"

"It's amazing! We're halfway. Today we get to experiment with bouquets and different layering techniques."

"Sounds like we might have to expand the flower garden to accommodate the budding florist," he said excitedly.

"I'd love more flowers here. We could plant daisies, forget-me-nots, and a rose garden. And, of course, poppies, my favorite."

"Sounds perfect, dear. I'll pop past the markets this morning and pick up some seeds. It will give me a break from the garden."

"That's okay. I can get them on my way home today."

He tilted his head to the side and smiled. "I know you can, but let me, please. I don't have a son here to spoil. Let me do this for you."

I nodded. "Thanks, Al, I'd love that."

He threw me a satisfied smile that reached his weathered eyes.

"Maybe I can make us some homemade pasta for dinner?" I offered, dusting the dirt from my hands.

"With your delicious basil pesto? I'll pick some fresh basil."

"Deal."

Al leaned back on his haunches and turned to me. "You never told me about New York, Lily, and it's been over a month since you came back."

I continued with my hands in the dirt, avoiding his gaze.

"I told you. Kit surprised Jazzie, buying her a karaoke bar. I mean, who does that… seriously!"

"A rock star?"

I nodded in agreement. "True."

"But that's not what I meant, Lil, and you know it." Gingerly, he stood so we were at eye level.

Fuck.

That was the first time in a long time I'd heard Al speak in a different tone.

A weight leveled onto my chest. Remembering Blake's lips on someone else's, his stony stare into the black cab, and how my throat clogged with emotion, I had buried the pain since returning.

"I took the address you gave me and caught a cab there. I was about to get out when he pulled up."

"So you saw him? You saw my son?" Al bounced from foot to foot, his weary face replaced with jubilance.

I stopped and glanced up at him. "I thought I told you that."

"No. And I didn't press you."

I twisted my lips, guilty for not telling him what had happened. "I saw him, yes. He was with a woman. They were all over one another. I just couldn't…" I quickly turned around when tears pricked the backs of my eyes.

"Oh, Lily." I felt a hand on my back, comforting me.

"I'm fine, really." I got busy in the opposite garden bed, angry with myself for letting Blake claw his way back into my life.

"My son has made me so proud, but I just want to whack him across the ears for whatever he did to you."

"It's fine. It was six years ago, Al."

"I know, but honestly."

I let out a long exhalation. "Honestly, I've cried enough tears over your son to last a lifetime. I'm so over it, and seeing him in New York just cemented that. I'm sorry I couldn't talk to him."

"Don't you dare apologize."

"You should be happy for him, Al. He looked like he had it all together. Has he called you lately?"

"Yes, just last week, which was nice."

My shoulders stiffened into tense balls. "You didn't tell him I was in New York, did you?"

"No, I promised you I wouldn't."

"Thank you." A sigh escaped my lips as my grip loosened around the rake.

"We had a good old yak, actually." He dusted off the dirt on his worn shorts, his face awash with pain. "But there is something you should know." Al steeled a glance my way, and my throat bobbed. I held his firm eye contact and pretended to act like whatever he was about to tell me didn't matter. "What's that?"

"Well, there's no sugarcoating it. Blake got engaged."

The rake fell from my hands as pain clawed at my rib cage.

Blake's engaged.

"Is that so?" I folded forward, picking up the wayward tool off the grass.

"I thought you should know, Lil," he continued.

The beautiful woman sucking face with him at his doorstep… *that was his soon-to-be wife?*

Nausea swirled around in my stomach. So much for moving on. The news felt real and raw, like the day he left me.

"Well, tell him congrats." I pierced the dirt with holes, taking out of my frustration on my unsuspecting ground.

"He asks about you all the time, Lily."

"Yeah, well, that's nice. What would be nicer is if he hadn't left me after his graduation party and never spoken to me again." Al shook his head in disgust. "Anyway, this has nothing to do with you, Al. I'm sorry, it's well in the past."

"He's recently been promoted again at that big-wig investment bank in Manhattan. All beyond me, but it sounds very fancy. Honestly, he sounds less and less like the happy-go-lucky Blake that I raised and more like a man with a mission to conquer the world."

I smiled. "Well, he always had goals."

"I just wanted him to be happy. And if that meant he had to leave Seaview to do it, then so be it." He pressed his hand on one knee and hoisted himself up. "I don't know what he did to you, Lily, but I'm truly sorry. You know that, right?"

"I know. And like I said. I'm fine. Now, let me dust off and get ready. I'll see you later tonight." I paused and caught his eye. "Perhaps without the Blake chat?"

"Deal."

Hugging Al goodbye, I set off toward the white weatherboard cottage. Roses spilled from the hessian garden beds, and the windows opened into the sunroom where my pottery dishes and pots colored the window frames. But all that color appeared like ebony and ivory.

The news pierced my heart. Blake's engaged. He had well and truly moved on. And all the boyfriends I had since him, I was kidding myself, thinking they'd help me move on. Seeing him in New York and now this brought all the heartache bubbling to the surface.

It was six years ago. *Why couldn't I move on like him?* But to him, it was nothing. *We were nothing.*

He was my everything.

3

BLAKE

My floor had cleared out. No longer were the phones buzzing or monitors on tabletops glaring with charts and numbers. Wall screens flickered with overseas markets that were trading live. Silence filled the room on the fourteenth floor that my team of traders and analysts had occupied. Even my Senior Product Manager, Carl Soder, had fucked off, leaving me to finish reviewing the billion-dollar fund we managed and its alignment with company strategy. But that wasn't new.

Carl quickly realized I wasn't like his predecessor, lazy as fuck. So he'd regularly let me run meetings with potential investors, which, at my age, was a no-no. But results meant more than adhering to company policy. I was bringing more money into our fund than anyone else, so he let me run with it while taking all the credit. Since becoming a portfolio manager, our initial targets had been smashed, and they now tasked us with running the largest fund in the company.

Carl, who was theoretically my boss, was a lazy prick and was all that stood between the Big Boss Club and me. I knew his MO, and it was only a matter of time before I took his job, and he was licking out my asshole.

Like him, most of the team were lazy, self-entitled rich kids. Hired by the hedge fund because of their trust fund parents, they did the smallest amount to get by and had expected the world to fall at their feet. I'd been surrounded by this type my entire life and fucking loathed them.

Jackson and Roche Hedge Fund was one of the newer hedge funds in New York. They'd taken me in when I hadn't even finished my economics degree at a public college in Manhattan. And out of the two hundred strong applicants vying for the same position, they picked another guy and me. He had since quit, but in six years, I'd worked my way up from being a nobody to a name people fucking respected.

Starting as an analyst, it only took a year for them to notice I was different. A mathematical whiz and problem solver from a young age, I was taught college-grade mathematics and economics in tenth grade. So when I pinpointed a fabricated balance sheet, saving the fund from losing hundreds of millions of dollars, Robert Jackson took notice. Part owner of the Hedge Fund Jackson and Roche, he swiftly promoted me, paid me a mega bonus, and added a few extra zeros to my bank account in the process. Hailed as the youngest twenty-five-year-old in the Financial District to ever lead a team, I worked crazy hours, hit the gym, and fucked like a machine.

My phone vibrated in my suit jacket pocket. "Blake here."

"Get your butt up here, now." Robert Jackson's tobacco-laced voice boomed down the line.

"Sure. Everything okay?"

"It's about Camille."

Fuck me.

New York socialite, Robert's daughter, and my fiancé.

What the hell had she done now?

Since moving in together, Camille's over-the-top personality and excessive partying were in plain sight. It was more bearable when we'd lived apart, but I guess it was something I needed to get used to now that she was my fiancé. That and the fact she wanted to change the furnishings and furniture I bought when I moved into my Upper East Side apartment put me on edge. Not because I didn't trust her choices but because she'd easily squander a hundred grand on a table and chairs after a visit to designer, Boca do Lobo.

"Okay, I'll be right up."

The line went dead, and my shoulders stiffened. *What had she done now?*

When I proposed last week and the announcement was made, I think it was the first time I'd seen Robert smiling.

The elevator doors closed, and I punched in the code to the executive floor. It ascended closer to the top floor, and music and laughter echoed. Another party on the private floor to end the week. Nothing new in our line of work.

The doors opened into the dimly lit, vaulted room, bordered with leather couches and ornate brass tables. Original oil paintings donned the paneled walls while a Swarovski crystal chandelier hung witness to the debauchery below.

The spice-laden cigar smoke snuffed out the oxygen, and my eyes took a second to adjust. Men in dark suits, plates of white powder, and women in lingerie filled the room. Women were everywhere, at least four to every man in the room. The sound of men racking up on the tits and asses of women was so common it didn't make my head turn. Dark corners didn't matter. Married men didn't need to hide here. This was the executive team—men who made tens of millions of dollars in their sleep and had beautiful women and coke for miles.

Jordan Belfort, eat your heart out.

"There he is. The employee of the year." Daley, VP of operations, took his head out from between a pair of tits.

"Daley." I gave him a knowing smile. Then my gaze flicked

to the blonde straddling him. She sucked on her lips as she eye fucked me. *Yeah, think of me while you fuck a man three times your age with saggy balls.*

"Do you know where Robert is?" His head returned to the woman's fake rack, wiping his nose across the white powder.

She giggled as he vacuumed the white dust between her buoyant tits.

"Fuck yeah." He wiped the tip of his nose with the back of his hand. "In his office.

I nodded, making my way toward his office. My dick swelled against the seam of my zipper at the sight of tits and ass. Damn, when was the last time I fucked Camille?

"Blake, in here." A voice sounded from behind the door. Slightly ajar, I saw the wiry frame of Robert behind it.

His voice cut through the beat of the sleazy sex club that I'd just walked past.

On the door to his office were the words 'Big Boss Club,' the club I'd worked my ass off to join.

"Rob." I inched the door open. Since proposing to his daughter, it changed to a first-name basis with him.

"Shut the door, son."

The door clicked shut, and I turned to the sucking noise in the corner of his office.

Two women, one with midnight blue lingerie and the other in a red collar and lace thong, lay across his couch. Both looked up briefly and collectively eye fucked me. Then, the one in blue squeezed the other's tits and licked her lips, keeping her eyes on me.

Fuck. I really need to fuck Camille.

I gazed over at Robert, who seemed completely oblivious to their presence. Robert married the love of his life, Caterina, thirty years ago. That's what the society pages said. They had two children, Camille and the heir to his fortune, Cambridge Jackson.

"So, let's talk about Camille."

"Right."

I sat down on the leather chair, waiting for his latest complaint about his daughter. Yes, she was a goddamn handful. Recently, she'd been burning through more cocaine than Pablo Escobar.

Inviting me to one of the firm's charity dinners was where he'd introduced me to Camille. Not long after, his pushy ways paid off. Not like it was difficult. Blonde, slim, and strikingly pretty, Camille was crazy wild and not just between the sheets. It wasn't too hard to fall into dating, then a marriage of convenience.

"She's absolutely everywhere. I set the two of you up, so she could get out of the society pages and settle down. In turn, you get to cement your reputation in one of the world's leading investment firms and our family. You're fine while my daughter is…" He shook his head.

"She moved in with me recently. We're engaged. Hopefully, that will settle her down."

"She needs a goddamn intervention." He slammed the table with his flat palm. "Does she need to go back into rehab?"

"No. She just likes to party. The only thing she's addicted to is the show."

"Maybe."

What do you expect? Camille started drinking and doing drugs younger than Drew Barrymore, thanks to absent parents and a shit-ton of money.

"All I know is last weekend she was pictured in a Soho nightclub with her tits out, high as a fucking kite. Where were you?" He glared at me, pinching the bridge of his nose.

"Here. I'm always here long after Carl leaves."

He grumbled. He couldn't have it both ways, and to be fair, I preferred to be here. Lately, Camille was becoming more demanding and unpredictable. Maybe it was the five-carat ring I put on her finger, or maybe it was because my townhouse wasn't what she was used to.

Smaller and not as luxurious as her mansion on Park Avenue, she wanted to change everything but the washers in the kitchen faucets.

"Well, once you're married, it has to stop. All of it. You can lock her up in your apartment for all I care. She's doing more damage to my reputation than ever before."

"And mine," I added.

A moan came from the women on the sofa, and my gaze fell upon them. The woman in the red collar circled the other girl's nipple with her tongue while she thrust her fingers inside her. *Fuck.* My dick thickened against the seam of my pants.

This life was strange but in the best way possible.

"Which one?" Robert asked, and I ran my heated gaze down both of them.

"Both are nice. I think you'll have a pleasant time with both of them."

The girl on top pouted her pillowy lips, the blue lace showcasing her pillowy skin.

"Which one do you want?" He steepled his hands on his desk, waiting for my reply.

Was he serious? I just proposed to his daughter. I didn't cheat. I knew how badly that could fuck someone up firsthand.

"I'm okay, thanks."

"Not what I asked." His glare held mine.

"Well, if I wasn't engaged to your daughter, I think they are both stunning, but the girl in the blue lingerie would be my pick."

"Katy, you heard the man."

The girl on top, the one who had been eye fucking me since I walked in, stalked over to me.

She sat on top of me, straddling me, her back to Jackson.

What the fuck? Was this a test?

I leaned around the girl as I watched a smirk spread onto Robert's face.

"Thanks, sweetheart, another time." I tapped her leg, and when she didn't move, I gripped her waist, lifting her off me as I came to stand.

Robert glared at me.

Fuck him. "If we're done here, I'm heading home."

"We're done," he snapped.

"See you tomorrow." I turned, walking toward the door.

"One last thing, Blake."

I glanced over my shoulder, the tapping of his fingers and his narrowed stare cornering me. "Set a date. The quicker she's in line, the quicker you'll become richer. You think this is a fantasy?" He waved his hand around at the women in the room. "Wait till there are extra zeros in your bank account."

Huh?

I nodded in agreement.

Uncertain of what just transpired, I meandered out of the lion's den and past the zoo of sweaty bodies. Then I exited the building and walked over to my waiting car. The mention of more zeros in my bank account was new. *Fucking new and fucking exciting.*

Big Boss Club, here we come.

"Home, Mr. Carter?"

"Thanks, Will."

Well, there was a first time for everything. And being offered a high-class escort from the man whose daughter you were engaged to definitely was a first. Sleeping around on your wives was acceptable and so commonplace here. Women turned a blind eye, spending their husbands' money on charity lunches at ten grand a pop or redecorating to pass the time.

But was that the direction I wanted to go down?

I stared out the window. As we drove through Lenox Hill,

tall brown buildings passed, and the sidewalk still bustled with people.

A blonde-haired woman walked past as we slowed down, and I craned my neck, apprehension knocking at my rib cage and stealing the breath from my lungs.

"Stop, Will," I yelled, and he slammed on the brakes, jolting me forward. I lowered my window to get a better look at the woman who looked so damn familiar it hurt.

I let go of the breath I was holding as disappointment flooded through my veins.

It wasn't her.

It wasn't Lily.

I squeezed my eyes shut, rolling my lips into a straight line.

"Everything okay, sir?"

When I reopened my eyes, Will was staring directly at me. It wasn't the first time I'd asked him to stop suddenly, and I knew it wouldn't be the last. Still, the guy must have thought I was losing it.

"Fine. Sorry, please continue."

We started moving again, and I couldn't let go of the pang of disappointment that shuddered through me.

When I had proposed to Camille, an image of Lily came into view. So overwhelmed by the unexpected vision of her blue eyes and bone-melting smile, I stammered my way through the proposal. Luckily, Camille was too blinded by the ring on her finger to even notice.

Every time I spoke with Dad, I asked about her. And each time, he gave me the cold shoulder for what I did to her. I couldn't blame him. I couldn't blame anyone for what had happened between us.

"We're here," Will said through the dividing screen.

I looked up and out the window. The awning glowed in the

darkness, the arched metal doors a statement in their own right. I'd bought into the newest, most prestigious block by award-winning architect, Frederico Zappia.

"See you tomorrow morning."

"Make it five-thirty. I have lots to do," I stated as I got out.

"Yes, sir."

Punching my code into the elevator, I was grateful to be home after the long week at work. And after seeing the sleuth of half-naked women, I was so randy my dick was about to fall off.

Having Camille move in had its perks. Whenever she was home, it was sex on tap. In fact, that's all we really did. But since working on an important deal at work, we'd hardly done that.

The doors opened, and I placed my bag down by the entrance. When I walked inside, a dim light by the library was on, but there was so sign of life. She must be out. Dammit, I'd have to sort myself out.

I flicked the light on in the kitchen. It was Friday night, just after ten. Normally, I didn't get in before midnight. My team was likely knee-deep in cognac and pussy at the private gentlemen's club downtown, but that was more their thing than mine.

I walked past the stainless-steel kitchen and toward the alcohol stand. Reaching for the scotch, I poured myself a fat two fingers and flopped onto the sofa, where I sucked back the golden-colored liquid. The more I drank it over the years, the easier it went down.

The thought of checking on Camille left as quickly as it came. She was a big girl. She could handle herself. And she was likely with Selina and Portia, both daughters of billionaires and equally troublesome. Plus, I was beyond exhausted. I stared vacantly at the traffic and crowds below, enjoying the silence from way up here.

A voice sounded in the distance. I thought it came from down the hallway.

What the fuck?

Lightly, I floated down the hallway toward the sound. But it wasn't a voice. It was a moan.

A moan I knew too well. *No fucking way.*

I arrived at the bedroom door, my blood raging with every step I took closer along the floorboards. Turning the brass handle, I pushed it open with a flick of the wrist. There, in the dimly lit light, I saw Camille's back. She rode a man like a bull, her blonde hair bouncing around like her fake tits.

I held my breath before even realizing what I was witnessing. "Am I interrupting something?"

She held the sheet to her naked body and whipped her head around.

"What the fuck, Blake?"

The man jerked beneath her. "Oh, shit."

"Get the fuck out of my house," I bit out, my voice dangerously low.

Next was a cacophony of sheets and naked bodies scurrying about. I watched as though everything was happening in slow motion. While he rushed for his discarded clothes, she sat with the sheet pulled up around her body, narrowing her eyes as I let off a deliberate exhale.

"I'm just going to… Camille… I'll see ya…"

"Call me?" she said.

Call me? Was she fucking high?

The man hopped into his shoes. I extended my foot, deliberately tripping the fucker over everything while keeping my eyes on Camille. He scrambled to his feet, not saying a word, and ran out the door.

"What the fuck, Blake?" she repeated, misplaced irritation lacing her words.

"Shouldn't I be saying what the fuck, Camille? You were fucking in our bed."

I slammed the door shut behind me and moved inside the room. It smelled of sweat and sex, and I wanted to puke.

"I fucking proposed to you last week, Camille."

"Stop pretending you care, Blake. You're never home. What did you expect?"

"I expect you to act like the perfect little wife and not fuck with my reputation."

She stared at her manicure and shrugged. "Don't tell me you want a real marriage. You don't love me, Blake, and I don't love you."

Love. I buried that feeling long ago.

"So, does that make what you did okay, Camille?"

You're marrying me to keep me out of trouble in return for career advancement. Everyone does it, Blake."

"Listen, it works both ways. I care for you, Camille, but this behavior has to stop."

"Who are you, Mother fucking Teresa?"

I shook my head and leaned against the back of the door. *What have I gotten myself into?*

She lowered the sheet, revealing her perfect tits. "What's love anyway? Love like my dad and mom have? He has his women and hidden families while Mama has her society pages and plastic surgery."

My mind went to the women in his office and the many before them. I puffed out my cheeks, remembering how the so-called love of his life ruined my dad.

Yeah, that's why I was in this arrangement in the first place because love is fucking overrated.

"Hello, Blake?"

Her voice pushed me into the now. "This has nothing to do with your parents. You need to grow up, Camille."

"Grow up?" She stood, dropping the sheet completely to

reveal a fresh wax. A grin curled into her cheeks as she strolled over toward me. *She was fucking dreaming if she thought I'd touch her after that.* Her arms snaked around my neck. She even smelled of his cheap cologne.

"Yes, grow the fuck up." I stared back at her.

She let out a haughty laugh, and a vein throbbed in my neck.

"Let's be real. I know why you proposed, Blake. Daddy needed me out of the papers. And what better way to do that than marry me off with his latest prodigy? *'Hedge funds' latest it-man, Blake Carter.' The Wall Street Journal*, right?"

"Robert called me his prodigy?"

"Fuck, you're just as bad as he is. What has he promised you? The fucking lodge in Aspen or the house in St. Barts? I'd be careful who you get into bed with, Blake."

"Careful who *I* get into bed with?" I stepped away from her and marched over to the window.

Staring out of the floor-to-ceiling glass, I watched the cars below as blood shot through my veins at lightning speed. Everything was perfect and shiny like the castle I lived in, but fractured limbs lay behind closed doors, and the same went for marriages.

Were all marriages meant to be a mask? A perfect image built on lies and cracks before it even started?

Her hand fell on my shoulder, and I grabbed it, pushing it away. "Your father is my boss, Camille. Apart from cementing my career here at the firm, he hasn't promised me anything." At least that part was true. It was only tonight, in his office, that Robert had offered me extra zeros. My guess was it would be a prenup condition. Prior to that, I'd earned it all.

Every fucking dollar.

Her perfect eyebrows raised into her forehead. "You're not stupid, Blake. Far from it. Otherwise, Daddy wouldn't have taken you under his wing and introduced us. He could have married me off to one of his millionaire friends, but instead, it was you."

"Hang on a minute. There was an attraction when we met. We've been together for a year."

She sniffed, clearing her running nose, and shrugged. "Sure, there are some feelings. You're gorgeous as fuck and have an amazing dick."

"Jesus Christ, Camille." I raked a hand through my hair.

"I call it how I see it."

"You know what I see? A rich little girl who was fucking someone in our bed." I kicked a cheap sock off the carpet. "Marrying me isn't some kind of reality show, Camille. You need to take some responsibility instead of blaming your parents for everything."

"A ring won't change a thing. Don't take it personally, but monotony is boring." A bemused smile reached her smudged lips, and I stepped closer to her, feeling my chest warm with agitation.

"Who the fuck speaks like that, Camille?"

"Me, I guess."

I crossed my hands across my chest, shaking my head and what I was hearing. "How many, Camille?"

She shrugged at the question. "I don't know."

"Fuck me," I bit out, baring my teeth. *Who was I marrying? Thank fuck I wore a rubber.*

"I will not change. Neither you nor Daddy can make me. If I want something, I take it. Be it diamonds or a man eye fucking me at a club."

"You're crazier than I thought."

"Maybe I am. But that won't change your mind from marrying me."

I narrowed my eyes, steam pouring from my ears. "How can you be so sure about that?"

"Because I know if you leave me, you can kiss your career

goodbye." I simply glared at her. Camille knew she had me with that statement alone.

Sure, love was overrated, but I thought we had an arrangement. One I sealed when I proposed. Fucking around and ruining my reputation in the process was not part of the deal. I never cheated on her, not fucking once. And boy, I could have, many fucking times.

The silver tray of white powder caught my attention, and I marched toward the side table. I picked up the tray, distaste swirling in my mouth. "Get rid of this crap. You know I don't like it in the house." I pushed off the plate, and it tumbled to the floor. White powder scattered all over my wool rug.

"Jesus, Blake." She ran to the powdery mess, trying to salvage what was left.

It was fucking pathetic. "Don't ever do drugs here again."

I walked out and slammed the door shut, leaving my naked fiancé in our room that smelled of middle-aged man and rank sex. I balled my hands into a fist and slammed it into the elevator button.

With every floor I dropped closer to the lobby, my skin burned with rage. I kicked my shoe against the skirting in the elevator, unable to hold the building pressure. A scuff now evidence of my wrath. *Christ, let them bill me for it.*

Is a lackluster marriage all for show what I want? What if we had children? I cringed at the type of mother she'd be.

The doors to the elevator pinged open, and I stepped onto the shiny marble floor.

"Evening, Mr. Carter. Can I offer you an umbrella, sir?" Ray, the concierge, greeted me.

"Think it might hold out for me, Ray," I replied.

"Sure thing, sir. Enjoy your walk."

As I walked through the archway of the door he held open for me, I gave him a curt nod. Then I stepped down the few steps onto the street and let out a loud exhalation. The weather, although freezing, was still warmer of late. I headed north along Lexington toward Central Park, going about the motions to clear my head.

Always rational and pragmatic, never emotional. Since leaving Seaview, I'd made that my focus. Emotions held you back. I wouldn't be at the dizzying heights of my career had I not left small-town Seaview when I did. Now, more than ever, I needed that cool head. I needed to be a realist and think this deal through, which was actually what it was.

It wasn't a marriage.

It was an arrangement.

And she needed to keep her end of the bargain. Fucking around and keeping drugs in my house was not it.

I loved New York. The relentless pace, endless possibilities, and the sour smell of hot dog flesh rotating on the nightly corner stand were everything I ever wanted. And I'd fucking made it. I was here. I was wealthy beyond my own dreams in a job I loved. *So cementing my future by marrying Camille made sense, right?*

Kicking a stone, I sent it rolling across the sidewalk and hit a woman's shoe.

"Hey, watch it, dickwad."

Except for that.

I was still getting used to the New York rudeness. I think it was born out of impatience rather than an actual notion of being rude.

"Sorry." I smiled.

She looked up. Her angry face melted away the moment her hazel eyes connected with mine.

I could fuck around like Camille. I had before I met her. *So why not now?*

There was nothing holding me back, not a ring and not an arrangement. But something still felt off about cheating. And it wasn't because I had feelings for Camille. Growing up with a father who loved a woman who cheated and left him left its mark on me. But no one could be hurt if neither were invested.

I smiled back, then kept walking. I was a good fuck, a fancy face, and a fucking genius. I certainly didn't have any problems getting laid. But getting laid all the time without committing to someone was a lonely life.

The only person to ever fill that void flashed before my eyes when I proposed to Camille. In that moment, when I glanced up from a bended knee, I saw Lily's ocean eyes, and the loneliness disappeared.

I pressed my eyes shut for a second. *It would never have worked with Lily.*

My phone vibrated in my jacket pocket, and I stopped on Lexington. I slipped it out of my inner pocket. *Unknown number.* Fuck, I hated unknown numbers.

Ignoring it, I shoved it back in my pocket and continued toward Central Park. I'd only progressed a few more steps forward when my chest vibrated again. I let out a throaty groan, and I slipped it out. Again, it was an unknown number.

Swiping the screen, I snapped, "What?"

"Mr. Blake Carter?"

Was that an Australian accent?

"Yes, this is he."

"This is Jenny from Seaview Emergency Department. I'm sorry to be the one to tell you this, but your father has passed away."

4

LILY

The bouquet of white lilies and juniper berries I meticulously arranged was splayed across the coffin.

Al. The only father figure I had since moving to Seaview was dead.

I wiped the tear that escaped from my eye.

The priest opened his worn Bible. The air was cool. The earthy smell of dirt and freshly mowed lawns filled the cemetery. I stared upward to the sky, and sadness slashed at my chest. The grief of losing my own father hit me like it was only yesterday. The car accident. Me in the back seat arguing with Mom and Dad to change the music. He took his eyes off the road for a second. A second was all it took to swerve on the slippery road and launch into a tree. They didn't stand a chance.

Al saved me. So did Blake. I could have so easily fallen into deep despair, but they rescued me. And now, in an instant, another person I loved was gone. *Just like that.*

A week ago we were talking about redoing the garden together. I set off to my floristry course on a sunny fall morning. But when I'd been on a break, my phone buzzed. Seaview's Emergency Department left a message to call them back.

Found on the side of the road just out front of the garden shop, he had gone to get my flower seeds like he said he would. Only he never returned. I went to the hospital, but it was too late. Pronounced dead on arrival. Cardiac Infarction. *Why don't they just call it a fucking heart attack?*

I left with his possessions in a black bag—a frayed wallet, a key ring with a hand-carved cross, and six packets of seeds. *My fucking seeds.*

They lowered the pine coffin into the dirt. Handpicked by Al himself, it was nothing fancy, just a tapered box. That was Al. No need to appear fancy when all the good stuff was on the inside. The man had organized his own funeral on one of those prepaid plans years ago, most likely because his son was across the other side of the world. Or maybe he knew I'd sell everything to give him the best send-off I could.

The priest closed the Bible. "I invite you to say your last goodbyes."

I stepped forward, leaving the comfort of Amber and Jazzie beside me, and picked up the single long-stemmed white rose. Then, carefully, I tossed it into the lowered coffin.

Goodbye, Al. Thank you for saving me from myself—twice. Not a day will go by that I never think of you. Damn, I'll miss our chats in the garden.

A warm tear ran down my cheek. I reminisced about the times we shared talking about gardens and woodwork and the fatherly knowledge he so carefully imparted without sounding like a father at all. All the things that filled my heart with joy.

My gaze drifted to my forearms, which had unexpectedly burst with goose bumps. My line of sight lifted. Blake Carter stood on the other side of the coffin. Taller and more muscular than I remembered with dirty blond hair in place of the whiter blond. *Had he been here this whole time?* He placed a single white rose next to mine, and with his shoulders slumped and his head low, he stood by his father.

He was wearing a navy suit, a thin tie against a crisp white shirt. He bent down, placing his hand atop the coffin, a silent whisper exchanged between father and son. A moment later, he rose to stand, and his gaze lifted to me as he did. We locked eyes. The hairs on the back of my neck stood at attention. And everything about that night came rushing back—his hands everywhere, our mouths desperately claiming one another.

Jesus, fuck. Here of all places. Sorry, Al. I'm going straight to Hell.

A hand around my waist tightened, and the hand on my shoulder squeezed in a comforting gesture.

My skin prickled as his stare waned. His brow furrowed, his green eyes tainted with sadness. I exhaled, the first to break the stare. Eventually, we would have to talk but not here and not now.

Even after the hell he put me through, I ought to tell him how truly sorry I was for his dad's passing. Then at some point, I'd have to address the need for new digs. Blake would sell this place in an instant to return to his fancy life in New York. *Fancy.* That's how Al had described it.

"Go in peace, Alistair Carter, and fly with the angels." Father Bogdov finished the ceremony with the sign of the cross.

A hand squeezed my shoulder again, and I turned to see Jazzie, who pulled me in closer. On my other side, Amber held my hand. Now, more than ever, I loved these girls.

Jazzie and I were instant besties as soon as I started at Seaview High. And it was at college we met Amber, who fit in perfectly. They were friends that stuck by you through thick or thin and didn't up and leave you when you needed them most.

Jazzie flew back from her new life with Kit in New York as soon as she'd heard of Al's passing. Amber left work immediately, taking three days off to be by my side and help plan everything—and Amber never took time off work—even a recent bout of pneumonia didn't stop her.

I wiped away another tear that rolled down my cheek, leaned into Jazzie, and squeezed Amber's hand.

When I stepped forward, all eyes in the crowd fell on me. "Thank you all for coming. I'd like to invite you back to Alistair's home for the wake and some light refreshments. He would have wanted us to share stories of the man who touched so many lives."

I glanced up at Blake, his lips lifted into the slightest of smiles. Expressionless, I gave him my back and leaned into the solace of my friends.

"Are you okay?" Amber asked, her brown hair smoothed into her signature top bun.

"I'll be all right. Thanks, girls, for coming. I love you both." I hugged Jazzie.

"Love you, sister from a different mister." She gripped me back.

"All right, let me in, you two." Amber jostled between us as we opened our embrace.

"I'd be lost without you guys." I exhaled.

"Me too," they replied at the same time.

Amber released me first. "Come on. We'd better go if we're going to get to the wake before everyone else." She was never one for showing too much emotion.

"True, it's not like Blake will be helping," I admitted.

Jazzie and Amber exchanged glances.

"What?" I asked.

"Did you see how he was staring at you after he placed the rose?" Jazzie asked.

Yes, I did.

"It was the first time he'd seen me in six years. Maybe I look different. I'm with bangs and a short bob now."

"You don't believe that." Jazzie ran a hand through her red hair and popped an eyebrow in question.

"Or maybe he realized he fucked up the best thing ever." Amber shook her head.

"Doubtful. He's in a committed relationship." I stopped short of telling them he was engaged. I just couldn't today.

"Since when?" Jazzie asked. She stopped walking, but I continued across the patch of dewy lawn. There wasn't any point dragging up the past, especially when they bore witness to the weeks and months of misery that followed after he left.

I shrugged, not wanting to make a big deal out of it, even though my insides were screaming out in protest. "It was one of the last conversations I had with Al."

"Christ." Jazzie caught up to me and was now scanning for my reaction. I wasn't going to give it to her. Nor to myself.

Blake Carter was the past.

"Well, fuck him," Amber added, looping her hand into mine.

A smirk peeled onto my lips. *Damn straight.*

"Amber, shut that potty mouth, for God's sake. We're at a cemetery!" Jazzie glanced around, checking if anyone had heard her.

"Well, should you be saying for God's sake then?" Her plucked eyebrow rose half an inch toward her forehead.

We all laughed. "Good point."

We fell into step, and I continued, "Anyway. Like I said, yes, he hurt me, and yes, I'm over it. And obviously, so is he. He was over it the day he boarded that flight to New York. Let's just be done with the wake. Then I don't have to see him ever again."

The exchanged glances between Amber and Lily didn't leave my peripheral vision, but I ignored them. I pushed on with every step as we approached the car. I had moved on.

"So, this outfit of yours today. You're telling me you didn't plan this because you were seeing Blake?" Jazzie pressed.

I stared down at my dress, momentarily forgetting what I wore. Everything in my wardrobe screamed color, so I picked the most muted dress I could find—a lilac sweetheart dress to the knee with tiny blue flowers that, from a distance, could be mistaken for polka dots. It was demure yet quirky, just my style.

"I don't own anything black. What would you rather me wear, my red overalls?"

Reaching the car, I opened the door and slid inside. I couldn't hide my irritation, slamming the door shut and nestled into my seat without waiting for a reply.

Five minutes later, we arrived at the house. An ostentatious bunch of flowers lay at the front door. "Wow, look at those." Jazzie pointed to the display.

The bouquet was extraordinarily large, almost bordering on gaudy, with red roses, white lilies, and baby's breath.

Closing the car door, I made my way toward the front of Al's house. Between the roses, I found an envelope.

Blake Carter.

Well, I shouldn't be surprised. I figured it didn't look like it'd be from anyone around here. Probably from his fancy New York family. I shrugged, turned my back, and steamrolled toward my cottage.

I walked through the open door. "Hi, Priscilla." The sweet aroma of onions and smoky bacon filled the cottage. My neighbor, Priscilla, who bought Aunt Josie's house, had kindly offered to set up the food so it would be ready when people started to arrive.

"Lily, how did it go?"

"As expected." I let out a loud exhale, and she curled an arm around my shoulders.

She pulled me into a hug, and I embraced her, frustration rather than sadness clawing at my chest.

She put the final touches on the food platters I'd prepared earlier while checking the oven. "I've got the rest of it heating in my oven because yours wasn't working properly."

"Oh, thank you." I rolled my lips on in themselves. "Al was going to look at that this weekend."

She scanned my face, and her expression turned pained. "I'm okay." I sighed, then patted the tops of my cheeks, willing the tears to roll back in.

Jazzie and Amber appeared in the doorframe. "You okay, hun?" Amber asked.

I nodded. "Just memories."

The creak of the side gate caught my attention. The low chatter of people started echoing around the garden, and I stood, steeling myself for the afternoon. "Jazzie, can you…"

"On it," she replied immediately, reading my mind.

Jazzie headed toward the groups of people and directed them toward the white marquee Amber and I had erected. Large, with plastic arched windows, we'd filled it with tables covered with floral tablecloths.

It was a sight to behold. The last time I had seen the marquee constructed was on Blake's eighteenth birthday. Another night etched in my memory, one where I saw him kiss Addison White under the fairy lights.

"Thank you," I yelled behind her.

"What can I do?" Amber asked.

"Can you fill those two jugs with water and cut some sliced lemon." I pointed to the ribbed set of jugs on the counter, and she nodded. "Blueberries in that jug and the lemon in the other."

"No probs." She shouldered out of her black blazer and got straight to it.

I'd be lost without my girls.

"I'll pop back soon with the quiches from the oven."

"Thanks, Pris, you're a lifesaver."

She winked. "He was an amazing man, Lily. It's the least I can do."

I inhaled and gazed out of my kitchen windows. Damn, I'd miss this place. The northern sun beat down on the emerald lawn. Passion fruit vines webbed the hardwood fence, and the sweet scent of lavender wafted into the kitchen from the nearby sea breeze.

People mingled, swapping stories of Al, how he was the resident handyman and carpenter, and how the local fire brigade had him on speed dial to rescue stray cats. His nickname was the cat whisperer. Still, to this day, we don't know how he did it. The stories made me smile. How he and his son built the cottage without a single power tool. I sucked in a shaky breath at the mention of him.

Blake was around here somewhere, and I was trying to avoid him for as long as possible. *How was I supposed to face him in the middle of this grief?*

The stories continued with how Al had the strength to go on after his wife, Joanne, left him when Blake was only five years old. *Where was she?* I probably wouldn't even recognize her. The only photo Al had of her was in the living room. He never took it down and called her the love of his life. The handful of times he'd spoken about her, I often found it surprising. Instead of being bitter that she ran off with another man and left him to fend for himself, he felt regret. He couldn't be the man she needed him to be, and he took that on himself. Al loved and cherished her with every bone in his body. Blake, on the other hand, never mentioned her.

My gaze fell to the corner of the orchard. Blake leaned against the pear tree, speaking with Al's best friend, Patrick Bates.

He'd removed his jacket and tie and unbuttoned the top few buttons of his shirt, revealing his tanned chest. His muscles, perfectly rounded, pressed against his shirt. Damn, he was fine. If muscles were a sport, he'd win gold. It was obvious he worked on his body, diet, and lifestyle rigorously.

He was Blake but crisper.

Cleaner around the edges.

Harder.

The cut of the chiseled jaw and hypnotizing green eyes made me weak at the knees. I steadied myself, trying to shake myself out of my comatose state. The betrayal that lay underneath that well-put-together exterior was something I could never forget.

"Lily, how are you doing, dear?" Bessie, from down the street, placed a hand on my shoulder. "I know how much he meant to you."

"Hello, Bessie. Thanks for being here. I'm okay." Truly, I'd run out of tears to cry. "How are you? I know how much he enjoyed playing bridge with you every Tuesday."

"Oh, he was a shark, that Alistair. Such a jovial character. He made everyone laugh. You know he hadn't the slightest insight into the effect he had when he entered a room."

I smiled down at her. "I know. That's what was so great about him."

Heat pricked the back of my neck as the weight of a stare fell upon me. My gaze drifted to the man under the pear tree. His look was unreadable, indefinable, but so tangible from across the orchard.

Bessie followed my stare out the window. "So Blake's back. Do you know for how long?"

I blinked a few times, reality interrupting. "No. I don't know. I haven't spoken to him yet."

Her wrinkled face tilted. "That's odd, isn't it?"

"He must have flown in this morning, and I haven't had the chance with all this going on." I gestured toward the crowds of people, slowly filtering out after a few nibbles. Pretty much everyone in Seaview turned out for the farewell.

"If you need anything, dear, you know I'm only at the end of the street."

"Thanks, Bessie."

"You know you could always join us playing bridge. We will need another player."

"Bessie!" James, another fellow bridge player, shuffled toward her.

"I'll think about it. Thanks for coming, Bessie," I said, welcoming the interruption. Polite chitchat was one thing, but as the day was coming to an end, I was too apprehensive to truly commit to any convincing conversation.

"Well, it looks like it's finally dying down," Amber remarked as they followed me back into my cottage.

"Bad choice of words," Jazzie added.

"Shit, sorry."

"It's fine, really, guys. Why don't you get going? It's been a long day."

"And let you clean this up? You're dreaming."

"They're disposable plates. I'll manage just fine, Amber," I argued.

"Have you spoken to him yet?" Jazzie asked, keeping her voice low.

"Spoken to who yet?" His gravelly voice bounced around the white walls of my kitchen, eventually settling to the depths of my stomach.

I couldn't turn around.

"Blake," Jazzie said, her voice somewhat higher. "I'm so sorry about Al."

"Thank you, Jazzie."

My hands trembled as I picked up the leftover sandwiches.

"Hi, Blake, I'm Amber. My condolences."

"Thank you." I felt lasers boring into the back of my head as silence filled the room. Guess it was my turn now.

Shifting on my heel, he stood a yard from me. His sandy

blond hair not a hair out of place—his almond-shaped eyes were darker and more imposing than I remembered. "Blake."

"Lil." His eyes burned into mine.

Silence.

"Ah. So we have to go," Jazzie interrupted.

"Yes, we do," Amber added.

Grateful for the distraction, I turned toward them both, taking extra time to hug each of my friends goodbye. "Thanks for everything, girls."

The girls walked out of the kitchen, taking turns looking over their shoulders before disappearing out of sight.

Blake stood silently watching me, his tall figure casting a shadow over the kitchen counter. I'd forgotten just how tall he was. Then there was me, all of five-foot-nothing, stood tiny. But not helpless.

Blake put his hand on the counter that separated us.

"Sorry, Blake. I know what he meant to you." I fingered my short bangs, unable to look at him.

"Come here, Lil." His voice sounded low and authoritative.

I walked around toward him, under his command, immediately angry with myself for doing so. Then, coming to my senses, I stopped.

"What is it?" He raised an eyebrow. "I just wanted to hug you. I'm sorry too. I know he was a father to you like he was to me."

I sure as hell wasn't *that* girl. Being burned and heartbroken was no longer part of my DNA. I was twenty-four now, and I'd learned my lesson.

"You lost the right to comfort me when you left six years ago without a word."

"Lil, l I know we have things to talk about, but can't we put that aside just for today? I think we can both find comfort in each other." He opened his arms, and his eyes widened, not taking no for an answer.

I stepped closer, his arms engulfing my petite frame, my head against his rock-hard chest. He squeezed me, his hand on my upper back, and I wrapped my arms around his waist, unsure of where to touch.

Everything about it felt awkward but also right. The last time I was with Blake, I was naked, asleep in his bed. *Now this?*

I pulled away, clearing my throat. "Thanks. I'll miss Suggy beyond words."

"Suggy?"

"Surrogate dad."

He smiled, and it hit me in the chest. "That's right. I remember you used to call him that."

"I guess there are a lot of things you must have forgotten." *Shit, I just said that on the day of his dad's funeral too.*

His stare lingered, a smirk lifted onto his face, and I felt a familiar ache pull between my thighs. *Damn, why did he have to look like a Calvin Klein model?* Arrogant as hell and persuasive more than the devil himself.

Still, the man who hurt me was just layered in a body of sin and cloaked in designer threads.

5

BLAKE

Her blonde hair changed from shoulder-length to a bob with bangs. She had delicious curves to go with her slim body and larger breasts that could make a priest sin. But I could still feel the same heart underneath that smart mouth and tempting ocean eyes.

She'd done all this—the wake, the marquee, and the abundance of food. I hadn't even thought to do anything like this. Then again, I wouldn't have had the time, so I would have outsourced it all, but this was just the touch Dad deserved.

The yard, complete with the marquee and tables, was set up like a picnic at Central Park. Platters overflowed with colorful fruit and sandwiches with various fillings. Homemade quiches swayed me from my strict eating regime. I'd lost count of how many I'd eaten. My personal trainer would hail down the wrath of a hundred squats if he'd paid witness to my binge-fest.

"So, can I help with this mess?" I asked, changing the direction.

"No, I'm fine," she said, returning to the other side of the kitchen counter. "Actually, we are being rude. I think the last group of people is waiting to say goodbye."

I turned around, and she was right. A few of Dad's friends from the club and others I didn't recognize hovered near the cottage entrance.

"Right." She walked past me, her flowing dress carrying the scent of laundry and lavender invading my senses.

Just memories, Blake.

"Again, we are sorry for your loss, Blake." Patrick rested a hand on my shoulder. "Please call before you go back home."

Home. "Will do."

Extra quiches later and more goodbyes, I felt more exhausted than pulling an eighty-hour week at work. Arriving from New York via Los Angeles this morning, I was ready to get out of my suit and empty a bottle of scotch. But with the state of Dad's house, I wondered if he had any of life's luxuries in there at all.

How had it gotten so bad? He was so fit and handy when I left. Guilt washed over me like a foul stench.

A man with a black hat and poor-fitting black suit tapped me on the shoulder. "Blake, do you and Lily have a minute, please?"

"Yes, sure." I turned to find Lily walking back from the main house toward her cottage. "Lil," I yelled out.

It was as though time hadn't passed, and I was calling after her to beg her to stay longer instead of going home to her aunt's.

She turned, her eyes narrowed. Reality slapped me across the face.

Jesus, did she hate me that much?

"There's a man here." I turned to him. "Sorry, I don't recognize you."

"Anthony Waters." He extended his hand, and I shook it.

I watched as Lily walked back, my gaze falling to the swell

of her cleavage. A perfectly full handful like I'd remembered. *What the fuck, Blake.*

"Sorry, how did you know Dad?" I shifted my attention.

"I was his attorney."

Surprised by his admission, I asked, "Dad had an attorney?"

The man smiled. "Of course."

"What is it, Blake?" She crossed her arms across her chest, and I couldn't help but drop my gaze. When I looked back up at her, she was a woman scorned.

I cleared my throat. "This is Anthony Waters, Dad's attorney."

She turned to face Anthony, the scowl on her face disappearing. "Anthony, thanks for coming. I'm sure Al would have appreciated you being here. If you don't mind, I have a nice mess to clean up in the kitchen."

"Before you do, Lily, I'd like to talk to you both about Alistair's will." *Both?* I glanced down at Lily, who opened, then closed her mouth. "This concerns you too, Lily. He wanted you both present for the reading. Can you come to my office on High Street tomorrow at noon?"

I took the card he'd pulled from his double-breasted suit pocket. "Sure."

"But me?" Lily asked. "Are you sure?"

She chewed the corner of her thumbnail. *She still did that?* The tell-tale sign she was nervous. I knew it well. Especially when things changed between us, and she experienced every single first with me, she damn near chewed the entire nail off.

She spotted me staring and stopped.

"Yes, you too, dear. Al wanted you there."

"Okay." Her eyes diverted to the ground.

"See you both then." He shook Lily's and my hand before turning and heading toward the side gate.

"Ah, so I guess I'll see you tomorrow," Lily said, not meeting my gaze.

"Are you staying here?"

She narrowed her eyes at me. "Yes, Blake, it's been my home for years."

I knew that. Stop trying to keep her here longer.

"Right, yes, of course, it has. I'm obviously jet lagged and delirious."

The fact that work lumped me with a project while on the plane and I'd gotten zero sleep didn't help—heartless bastards.

"You know, I will take you up on that offer for help." A smile spread on her peach-stained lips, and my gaze lingered.

"Of course you will." I trudged behind her, back to her cottage. For fifty yards or so, we walked in silence. The marquee and tables were now empty and wiped clean. "Thank you for organizing this."

"Sure," she remarked dryly.

"I probably should have called."

Fuck. Wrong choice of words.

She swung the door open and whipped her head around, her piercing blues staring back at me. "What?"

Double fuck.

I swiped a hand through my hair. "I mean, I probably should have called after I got word of Dad's passing to help organize all of this."

And after that night we made love, and you trusted me with your virginity. The massive elephant in the room would have to be addressed at some point, just not now.

She exhaled. "You can start over there." She pointed to the stacked paper plates with half-eaten food scraps. "So wasteful." She shook her head. "If you are going to pick up food, then eat it."

"I couldn't agree more. These quiches were off-the-charts good. I think I ate about ten of them alone."

She turned, and a satisfactory smile lifted into her soft cheeks. Her eyes held mine and her tongue dusted her bottom lip as something swirled between us. The hairs on the back of my neck stood at the thought of pinning her to the wall, silencing her with a kiss.

I cleared my throat. "My trainer's going to punish me when I see him next."

"You have a trainer?"

"Of course. He comes to the apartment every day. Usually, it's at some ghastly hour, like four in the morning."

She shook her head. "That's ridiculous."

"I don't think so." I tossed the disposable plates into the rubbish bag. *Why did she think working out was ridiculous?*

"So, Al told me you're some big-shot hedge-fund guy." She kept her head down, intentionally avoiding me. *Was she mocking me?*

I laughed. "Sounds like Dad." Just saying his name, a fresh sadness swept over me.

"You could say that. I work for Jackson and Roche. Crowned youngest banker in Manhattan to increase a hedge fund's investment by over thirty percent in one year... you're looking at him."

"Yeah, that means nothing to me. What was the crown like?" she asked, her voice taking on a tart tone.

She *was* mocking me.

"No crown. They threw me a party and gave me my first million."

She fumbled with the platters, and the pitchers fell, clanging onto the pine floor.

Yeah.

She bent over to pick them up, my gaze drifting to her round ass. My dick twinged in my pants at the unholy sight.

"And you're engaged?" She grabbed the pitchers and threw

them in the sink. "Congrats," she said, scrubbing the pitchers vigorously.

Look at me.

"Thanks."

"Who's the lucky lady?"

The whore I caught swallowing up some guy's dick in our bed.

"Camille Jackson."

"As in the Jackson in Jackson and Roche?" Her ocean blues widened, feathered by a million lashes.

"Yes, as in that."

"Interesting." Her gaze diverted back to the sink and the scrubbing of platters.

"And what's so interesting about that?" My stomach hardened. I knew exactly what she was thinking.

"Never mind, it's not my place."

"Oh, but it is now." My voice fell low and challenging.

She turned on her heel, the water sloshing from her hands to the floor, which didn't seem to bother her. "Really?"

I lowered my gaze, blood throbbing through my veins. "Really, Lil."

"I guess I never pictured you sleeping your way to the top. That's all."

For fuck's sake, it couldn't be further from the truth. "You don't know anything about Camille and me."

I held her contemplative gaze. "You're right. I don't." She stuck her hands back into the dirty dishwater. "Well, I'm happy for you, Blake. If she makes you happy, then nothing else matters, does it?"

The question hung in the air between us like a lead balloon.

Did she make me happy? And what did happiness have to do with marriage?

6

LILY

My breath caught in my throat, and I released it as soon as Blake excused himself to the bathroom.

Okay, maybe I sounded like a bitch. I needed to peg it down. He was only here for—well, I don't know, a few days at best—and I was busting his balls. If it weren't for his dad's passing, I wouldn't have cared.

I rested my hands against the cool stainless-steel sink.

Just dial it back a little, Lil.

"Still talking to yourself, I see."

Shit! Did I say that out loud? It was a weird thing I occasionally did. I hoped to hell he hadn't heard me.

"Just tired, is all. I haven't had a moment to really think." *And I find you intimidating.*

"So, tell me about you?" He sat on the barstool, his stare drifting down to my lips, then up to my eyes. *Goddamn, was it hot in here?*

I threw him a tea towel. "Well, may as well do something while you're sitting pretty."

He caught the flying tea towel that hit his chest. "Yes, ma'am." He let out a throaty laugh.

Oh, how I'd missed that sound.

"What do you want to know?" *How devastated I was after you left me? Or how the way you kissed me stole the air from my lungs.*

"What did you do after school? Dad mentioned you went to college."

"I did. Well, I started, at least. Never finished my degree in digital marketing."

"How come you never finished?" He scratched at his dirty blond hair, the same hair I remembered raking my hands through *that* night.

I inhaled deeply, then released it. "Oh, I don't know. Just wasn't for me."

His thick eyebrows pinched together. "You're not giving me much here, Lil."

You could have picked up the goddamn phone years ago if you wanted to know me.

I bit the side of my cheek. "Right. I stuck it out a year in college. That's where I met Amber. Now she's truly an amazing friend. Took three days off to help me with the wake." I paused for effect, letting that hang purposely in the air.

A tension-filled expression crossed his handsome face.

"So I dropped out because it wasn't for me, and since then, I've been doing bits and pieces."

"Bits and pieces?"

Yes, goddamn, you only live once.

"Online consultancy work for marketing agencies, Pilates, floristry, anything I can get my hands on that interests me, really."

"Interesting," He polished the white platter in his hands repeatedly. The damn thing never looked so shiny.

"How's that?"

"I remember you loving animals. I just thought you'd end up being a vet or, I don't know, working with animals someday."

Images of Puss Puss, my black and white socked cat, flashed by. My parents bought Puss Puss on my sixth birthday from a rescue shelter. That furball with the unoriginal name was my everything.

When they were taken from me, so was the cat. Aunt Josie's allergies meant no pets, which was just another slash to the chest.

"You were so good with Camembert. He'd always go to you over me." He cocked his head to the side while remembering.

"That's because you hardly walked him, and he was your pet."

"He had half an acre to wander around in here!" He outstretched his arms, his corded forearms on display with his shirt sleeves rolled up.

The idea of his arms on my bare skin sent a spark up my spine. I sucked in a breath. He wasn't going to have this effect on me again. He'd be gone soon, and that would be that.

I cleared my throat. "Things change, I guess." I turned my back to him.

"I guess they do." I heard the stool drag across the wooden floor. "Well, if that's it, I think I'll call it a night."

I turned around. "That's it."

"Thanks again for today, Lily."

"Of course, no problem," I said hurriedly.

"Did you want to get a ride into town tomorrow to the lawyer's office?"

"Do you have a car?"

"No, but I assume Dad still has the pickup in the garage?"

"He does. I mean, he did," I corrected myself.

"Does that thing still run?"

"As good as ever, but he preferred to walk."

Like the final morning, he had walked into town for me.

Guilt found its way up my toes and into my heart. I looked up at Blake.

"Do you think if Al had chosen to take the pickup instead of walking into Seaview, he'd still be alive today?"

"I don't think we can think that. If he were driving and he'd had a heart attack, he could have run into a mother and a child too." Blake wrapped his hands behind his neck, rubbing it back and forth. "His time was up, although cut short at sixty-nine, he lived the life he wanted, and you can't do any better than that."

I sighed. "You're right. No good will come of it."

He stepped around the kitchen toward me, and my heart leaped into my throat. The next thing I knew, his strong hands were around me, pulling me in for a hug. *What was this? Were we friends now?* From friends to lovers, then back to friends? Awkward as fuck, I lifted my arms around his waist. Broad shoulders held me tighter and into his rock-hard chest. His scent was heavenly, like an expensive cologne and a dirty one-night stand.

He scanned my face, his hand tilting the base of my chin up so I was forced to look at him. "See you tomorrow."

"Sure." I swallowed down the lump in my throat. It seemingly was the only word I could muster out of my now eight-year-old vocabulary.

His eyes darkened, and something swirled between us. Quickly, he let go of my chin and walked out, leaving me in a puddled heap.

Okay, so what if I imagined his strong arms scooping me up into his chest, his lips trailing kisses down my neck while he expertly guided his fingers inside me?

I was human. But some things never change. He was still a leopard. And his spots were fucking permanent. Plus, *he was engaged.*

7

BLAKE

The plinking of water droplets woke me, but I wasn't in Niagara falls—far from it. I walked from my old bedroom that backed onto the kitchen to find the source of the problem. Well, one of them, at least. The kitchen with wooden doors that Dad had made was exactly how it was when I left years ago. I turned the leaky faucet all the way to the right, but it only slowed down the drip. I opened the cupboard below the sink, and the damn thing came away from its hinges and into my hands. *Fuck me.*

That wasn't the only thing in a state of disrepair. Inside the old weatherboard house, beige paint peeled off the walls, and stains littered the decorative ceiling roses. Lights were out, or at best, flickering. The tiles in the shower sounded hollow underfoot, and when I showered, I was either burned or frozen by the erratic water temperature.

But the place was clean and spotless. It would be a great renovation for a young family or couple who wanted a big block, moments from the seaside. But I'd have to let it go, which gave me a heaviness in my chest and limbs. Sure, I could keep it. I didn't need the money, but what would I do with a house when my life was halfway across the world?

I let out a heavy sigh. God, I'd miss this place. Everywhere I turned, a childhood memory came flooding back in. Last night, I roamed the house ending up in the garage, alone with two of Dad's treasures—the 1967 pickup truck and his lathe.

Running my fingers across the wood-turning machine, I wondered about the last time he used it. He'd spent his life as a carpenter and taught me skills I hardly used today. And when he wasn't working day and night, he turned wood. In time, he crafted our kitchen cupboards, wardrobes, and chest of drawers. He could upcycle discarded wood into treasures.

It was early, but the sun streamed in through the windows. Unable to sleep, I'd been up for hours taking a trip down memory lane, trying to let go. Eventually, I walked into his bedroom. His bed was made neatly, his glasses perched on his nightstand beside a book. He was always reading. I picked up the worn book. *Jane Eyre*. Damn, he still had not gotten over Mom leaving him. Reading romance was just plain torture.

I flopped onto his made bed, spreading my fingers out and feeling the soft duvet. The scent of him lingered in the stale air.

Fuck, I'd miss him.

The old man was it. He was the real deal. He was the reason I was where I am today.

A deafening silence would now replace our weekly phone calls. The stories of bingo and bridge he shared while he sipped on his sherry. The advice he so gently passed over to me when he didn't think I was listening. I rubbed my forehead. He was a good man. *No.* He was a *great* man.

I pulled myself from his room and walked out the back door. The glorious salty sea air replaced the musty-scented home. Strolling toward the orchard, I opened the ornate metal gate and picked a lonesome berry from the bush, popping it into my mouth. Damn, the freshness was so good. How I'd missed that. And helping myself to whatever was growing in the garden—something I took for granted as a kid, no doubt.

My phone vibrated in my back pocket just as a gust of wind sent copper star-shaped leaves raining down on me. I slid out my phone while dusting down my black polo shirt. Camille's name flashed on the screen, and I puffed out my cheeks, letting it ring out.

I'd left Camille in the same way I'd found her— indifferent. She said we were fine. She cared for me and was committed to marrying me. I ignored her, grabbed my passport out of my safe, and left for JFK.

"*As long as she makes you happy, son.*" That was the wisdom Dad imparted in our last conversation. Happiness was over-rated. Fleeting at best. Dad, of all people, should have known that the minute Mom chased another man's dick.

I kicked the stone in front of me, bouncing off the garden gnome and knocking it over. Picking it up, I couldn't believe he still had this fucker. His naughty garden gnome. With sunglasses and a lime-green mankini, Dad and Lily loved it. I was mortified when he bought it. I propped him back into the ground, digging him into his usual spot, and let out a chuckle.

My gaze lifted to the white-shingled cottage. Inside, Lily glided effortlessly back and forth from the kitchen, sipping her morning drink. She loved her array of teas when I first met her.

Who the fuck drank herbal tea at age fifteen?

It felt like forever since I left Seaview, but it had only been six years. Yet, staring at her smooth skin, blonde bob, and speckled cheeks took me back to a time when everything was right in the world.

With only a few weeks out from my graduation, the pull I had toward her had become stronger than the earth's gravita-tional pull. And an all-consuming secret kiss led to an unforget-table three weeks ending in me taking her virginity on a night etched on my brain. Leaving her like I did was a mistake and one I pushed into the crevices of my heart. But I'd just graduated from high school and had big goals. Goals that small-town Seaview couldn't give me.

She knew that. I hadn't lied about my intentions except for the part where I moved my trip up to the day after we slept together. I wasn't meant to leave for a few more months. I brushed her lips with mine in the still of the morning and quietly walked out, choosing my career over anything else.

Yesterday was the first time I'd spoken to her since that day, and she shone like pure sunshine on a cloudy day.

But the resentment I felt from her yesterday hurt. Her body was tense, her gaze either distant or angry. But when she did look at me, there was something there. Something about us was unfinished. It was likely my missing apology.

I'm sure that would fix things between us and all the awkwardness.

But watching her hovering about and making sure everyone had enough food and drink yesterday, Lily hadn't changed one bit. Except, if possible, she'd become sexier. Her blonde hair was shorter, more strawberry than I remembered. It curved under the line of her jaw, elongating her neck. Her bangs were just long enough to sweep across her eyes—huge intoxicating baby blues I could drown in all over again.

The kookaburras let out their territorial laughter, pulling me from my trip down memory lane—a nice change from the car horns and sirens that echoed in the streets of Manhattan. Soft waves of music rolled over me as my bones nestled into the carved-out timber seat.

Coming from the cottage was a cross between Café del Mar and house music. I let the sound wash over me as my entire body relaxed. Then I lifted my nose to the scent of sandalwood.

Was she burning incense?

Lily never fit the box of a normal teenager. As teenagers,

we all tried to conform so we didn't stick out. She preferred being the square peg. That's what drew me to her in the first place. She didn't care about fitting in, and I so desperately wanted to—getting straight A's and working my ass off to skip ahead while also being invited to Brennan's parties at his oceanfront house with the coolest kids and the hottest girls from school.

Why leave all that? It wasn't enough. It's not like I hated Seaview. I just knew my lot in life was bigger than this town, bigger than this city, and damn bigger than this country.

Even my feelings for Lily, my best friend, couldn't keep me here even though she was the hardest part of leaving.

A few beads of sweat appeared on my forehead—not entirely sure it was from the heat—I wiped them away with the back of my hand. I puffed out my black shirt that began to cling to the crevices of my chest.

Lily walked down the pebbled walkway toward me with two cups and saucers in her hands.

Dressed in leggings and a rainbow cardigan with a white camisole, my eyes drifted to the shell of her exposed shoulder where the cardigan had slipped.

"How long have you been sitting here?" she asked.

"I'm not sure."

"The garden does that to you."

A slow smile spread across my mouth. "Does it?"

Her eyes locked onto mine, and something swirled between us.

She set down the cup and saucer on the dried-out tree stump turned coffee table. "Here's a peppermint tea." The faintness of cherry red blossomed into her cheeks. I closed my eyes, locking in the scent of her, and when I opened them, she was staring at me.

"Thanks, but I only drink coffee now. No more herbal tea for me."

"Oh?"

"I need as much caffeine in my life as I can get working eighty to ninety-hour weeks." And I wasn't going to snort my life away to stay awake like the boys on my team. We turned a blind eye to that sort of thing anyway.

"Well, I guess we should go then." She picked up the tea and saucer and set back to the cottage. "I've got things to do, and I'm sure New York wants their hedge-fund prince back ASAP."

I let out a throaty laugh. "Yes, yoga waits for no one. Tell me, do you wear those tight yoga pants? I could just imagine them on you…"

She whipped her head around. "Actually, it's floristry. And yeah, my ass in those pants would melt your face off." Her mouth tipped up into a delicious smirk.

I sucked in a sharp breath as my lip licked across my bottom lip. O*h, the things I could do with that smart mouth.*

* * *

The pickup still ran like a dream. I missed the old thing. It rattled and purred, but under the engine, it was alive and kicking. It spluttered and coughed on startup, but the ride into town was brief, which was good, considering Lily basically ignored me the entire way.

Anthony Waters opened the door to his office. "Hello, thanks for coming."

The small carpeted space reeked of wet feet and stale air. Certificates framed in chipped gold frames hung on the wall behind a worn oak desk and next to a library of dusty books.

"After you." I gestured for Lily to enter ahead of me. She smiled slightly as she walked past me. When her arm grazed my forearm, she inhaled sharply. Her touch, coupled with her response, sent sparks of heat up my spine.

Just old feelings, Blake.

"Take a seat, please." Anthony sat in his swivel chair as Lil and I sat opposite.

I hadn't thought about Dad's will. I didn't want for anything, so this was a mere formality before I got on a plane back to New York.

Lily gripped the sides of the chair and contorted her lips like she used to when she didn't know the answer to something. She felt uncomfortable being here, but I didn't mind. Dad loved her like a daughter, so it made sense for her to be here.

"Alistair, as you know, didn't have many possessions. He was a simple man who lived every day as though it was his last." He opened the document in front of him and took a deep breath.

"This is the last will and testament of Alistair Fred Carter. Alistair bequeaths his 1967 Ford pickup truck to his only son, Blake. The remainder of his estate at 146 Rose Drive, Seaview, is to be left to both Blake Carter and Lily Stone in equal shares."

Lily whipped her head around. "Blake, no. I'm so sorry."

That was Dad, always thinking about others. He knew I had enough. I didn't need the house. She'd been with him when I was in New York. Lily had been his company nearly every day. "Don't be." I smiled at her and reached out, placing my hand on top of hers—warm and silky smooth. Her gaze drifted down to where our fingers touched, and I quickly moved my hand back to the side of my chair.

What the fuck was that, Blake?

"There's more, Blake, Lily." Fortunately, Anthony interrupted whatever the heck we had going on.

"You can do whatever you want with the house. After all, you both will own it. But, there is one condition. Blake, your father wanted you to remain in Seaview to renovate the house with Lily."

I laughed, but when his expression remained unchanged, I realized he wasn't joking.

"What?" I barely breathed out.

"For two weeks."

"That's crazy. That's not really in there?" I leaned over the desk, snatching the corner of the paper.

He pulled it back, and I screwed my face up in annoyance. "Yes, it is. I can show you this after we finish, Blake."

I slapped my hand down on the armrest. "I have a job, a life in New York. I can't take two weeks off. Dad would have known that."

What the fuck is going on here? *Had Dad completely lost his marbles?*

My mind cast back to our last conversation a week ago. I shook my head. Nope, he was sharp as a tack.

"I'm sorry. It's right here." He looked down at the fucking sheet of paper in front of him. If we weren't in such a formal setting, I would not have stopped until I had that sheet of paper in my hands.

"Well, what if I can't stay?" I could already feel my chest tightening.

"Then the house by default goes to Brennan Jones."

Had I heard him correctly? A vein throbbed in my neck. My eyes nearly popped out of their sockets.

"Fuck off, it does."

"What?" Lily gasped, causing me to turn. Her expression mirrored mine. She knew all about Brennan, the slimy prick he was.

"May I enquire as to who Brennan Jones is?" Anthony asked.

"Rich prick I went to school with." *That's all he needed to know.* He didn't need to know he drove me out of town. And he certainly didn't need to know I punched his nose in when he tried to kiss Lily. My Lily. The thought of her with him made my stomach turn. Actually, the thought of her with anyone but me made me sick.

Fuck! Focus, Blake.

"Why would Al have done that?" Lily shook her head, her hand resting on the base of her neck. In a moment of confusion and weakness, my gaze lingered on her exposed collarbone.

"Blake." My eyes collided with hers, pulling me out of my Lily-like trance.

"I don't know." I pushed my seat out and started pacing the length of his tiny-ass office.

"But I know this is fucked up. I can't be away from my job for two weeks. Just like he knew I wouldn't possibly ever give a nickel to that piece-of-shit Brennan." My hand fell into my hair, fisting it in anger as I slammed my other palm against the wall causing picture frames to rattle.

"Sit down, Blake, please." His voice was steady and firm. I didn't like it.

I looked across at Lily, who could read my fucking thoughts. She tilted her head and nodded, begging me to calm the fuck down.

I pinched the bridge of my nose and pushed out slow deep breaths, determined to find another way. It only took a moment for an idea to pop into my head. "I got it. How 'bout Lily renovates the house while I'm in New York, then we sell it and split the profits?"

Lily stared up at me. "Not to sound ungrateful by any means, Blake, but I have responsibilities too, you know."

"Like what, yoga?" I threw my hands up in the air. "Sorry, it's arranging flowers this week, right?"

She narrowed her eyes. "Don't be an asshole, Blake." Her tone clipped, she was still gorgeous as fuck when I made her mad. It was as though nothing had changed.

"Were you two always like this?" Anthony asked, shaking

his head. Without waiting for an answer, he continued, "That won't work, Blake. If you are not in Seaview for two weeks, the house automatically goes to Brennan Jones. It's in here, black and white."

I pushed my hand to my forehead. There's no way Jackson and Roche would let me sit out for two weeks. Not with everything happening at work. Then there was Camille. I had no doubt she'd occupy herself with the bellboy or the latest spring social event. But I couldn't give two shits about her.

"It's just two weeks, Blake." Lily's voice sliced through my thought, the annoying voice of reasoning she was.

"Two weeks is like a year in the job I have. You wouldn't understand," I snapped, not needing this shit right now.

Immediately I regretted my tone, but like always, I'd done the damage. She recoiled at my words, causing me to look up at her. Her bright blue eyes appeared cold and distant, making my stomach roll.

"You're right. I don't. But I do know it's what Al wanted. So it's your call, Blake."

My gaze drifted to the floor. The brunt of my anger shouldn't be directed toward her.

She pushed her chair out, extending her arm. "Thank you, Anthony. That was the last thing I was expecting, but please know I will do my best to make Al proud." Her glare flicked to me. "And if it's to fix up the house that was once his home, so be it."

I watched her walk out the door. She strutted in her platform shoes, her ass swaying deliciously.

Shit, she made me mad and hard.

"One last thing. He has a letter for you, Blake. He asked me to give this to you in private." He walked around the desk and handed me an envelope. I took it in my hands and looked down. Brown smudges appeared on the edges, and the envelope was slightly crumpled. In true Dad fashion, he'd probably scribbled it on a piece of leftover paper he'd found in the garage.

My chest constricted, a heaviness settling in. "Thank you."

"He said to read it after your two weeks in Seaview are up," Anthony added.

I rubbed my temples. "So I guess he knew I'd stay then."

"I guess so."

8

LILY

How dare he mock my choice of work? Millions of dust particles flew into the air. I banged the dashboard with a flat hand, letting out all my pent-up frustration. A cross between elation and annoyance throbbed through my veins.

Al left half the house to me? What a generous soul. He hadn't needed to do that. I was fine on my own, always had been. I didn't care for anything but the clothes on my back and a good old chat. He knew that.

Blake stalked back toward the truck, his head hung low. He climbed in, slamming the door shut. "Well, shove a fucking jackhammer up my ass. Now what?"

"This is news to me too, Blake." We sat in the parking lot, staring out at the Pacific Ocean. The ocean crashed, sucking back sand and seaweed, then throwing it back again. The gusty breeze shook the fall leaves off the trees, burnt-orange and rich maroon leaves see-sawed across the promenade, barely missing cyclists, as the silence stretched between us.

"This is perfect for you, Lily."

"How dare you?" I spat through gritted teeth. "I didn't ask for this."

He shook his head. "I know you didn't." His voice was almost a whisper, and I got the feeling he was sorry for his outburst.

"Why can't you just accept these were his last wishes? You could leave here for six years and not see your Dad or me, but you can't spend two weeks away from New York? What is so pressing you can't spend two weeks out of your entire life to fix up the house you grew up in, then sell it? If that's what you want?"

"I may have left, but I talked to Dad every week. I didn't just leave him. He couldn't fly, you know that. And selling the house is what I want." He lifted his head, meeting my gaze. "I don't have a need for a house here. My life is over there. My job, my career, everything."

"Your rich, beautiful, blonde fiancé?" I added, and our eyes locked, tension swirling between us.

"Yes, her too." He cast his eyes down, then quickly flicked back up. "Wait, how do you know what Camille looks like?"

Shit.

"Um, your Dad obviously told me about her in passing."

His hands tightened around the peeling steering wheel, and I wondered if there was more to that relationship than he wasn't telling me. One thing was for sure, he certainly didn't gush about her like someone in love would.

"Selling it would be a shame, but I'll leave that up to you. I don't feel like I'm able to make that decision anyway."

"I want to sell it. I need to go back to New York."

"Okay, then it's settled. Two weeks here. Then you're gone for good." I exhaled. "I'm happy to deal with the agent so you can go *home*."

"Right." His grip around the steering wheel grew tighter,

his knuckles stretching until his skin turned white. "I have to call Robert Jackson."

"Your boss, right?"

He nodded. "Fuck, he's going to rip me a new one."

"Well, screw him, Blake," I uttered. "If he can't understand that your father just passed away, then what kind of man is he?"

"He runs a billion-dollar hedge fund, and he's missing one of his key men. He's a businessman, Lily. A shrewd one at that."

"Sans the heart," I muttered. "Let's go. I'm hungry." I turned toward him, but he just stared vacantly at the horizon. "Blake?"

"Yes. Right." His eyes strained as he clicked the key into the ignition and turned it over.

Work was everything to him. I understood the need for money but giving your life to someone else for eighty hours a week just to see the inside of an office. *Fuck's sake.* I would rather be tied to a tree in the middle of winter, stark naked.

Coming from a modest upbringing, Blake always craved more, setting his sights on the bigger picture. And credit to him, he got there all on his own. It was nothing to sneeze at. But I got the feeling it all came first and, more importantly, before his fiancé.

The thought rolled my stomach. I momentarily closed my eyes, savoring the feeling of his velvety hand on top of mine in the lawyer's office. The warmth gave rise to hundreds of goose bumps on my skin as I remembered his lips on mine and magic hands on my skin the night I lost my virginity.

"I need something decent." He interrupted my wayward thought, and I shook away the ache pressing between my thighs.

"I can make us a sandwich? The ones—" I was about to

mention the sandwiches Al used to love me making, but he cut me off.

"I said, decent. Come on, my treat." He pulled out of the parking lot and sped up toward the south end of the ocean, around the corner to the group of shops behind High street.

"Fine." *Your loss.*

"Since when has Seaview gotten fancy?" He stared out at the rows of glass-fronted stores and cafés. Awnings separated each eatery as people spilled onto the street, filling tables and sipping on their almond lattes. It had changed a lot in the time he used to live here.

"Since people realized it was only an hour from the city and the best beach on the coast. The town's flooded with new money. People are calling it the next Byron Bay."

He slowed down, surprised by the variety of modern eateries that spilled onto the main street. "There's even a smashed avocado breakfast bar. Now you really know Seaview's on the map." He let out a chuckle.

Sarcastic prick.

He slowed down when he passed the shops to where, almost overnight, an eight-story exclusive hotel spawned from the ground up. "I didn't notice this on the way in yesterday."

"It's a new five-star hotel. By the way, were you late to your Dad's funeral?"

He glanced over at me. "Yes. You noticed that?"

"Uh-huh."

"My plane was late. But I chartered a helicopter from the city to make up for the lost time. I was five minutes late if that."

I turned to him. *Who are you, Blake Carter?* "Well, lucky they had one on standby for you."

He flashed me a grin, his wonky bottom tooth no longer crooked and straighter than an arrow.

"There was no way I was going to be late for the old man

who did so much for me." He glided the truck into a spot effortlessly, leaped out, then walked around to my side, moving like he was in slow motion.

Fitted pants gripped his tight thighs, and the black polo top clung to his biceps, his corded arms on display. Short stubble adorned his angular jaw as he ran his hand through his dark-blond hair, taming it from the gust of wind that swept it across his olive complexion.

He opened the door for me, his green eyes intense. "Let's go, Lil."

"Sure," I squeaked out, ignoring the image of running my hand up and down his riptide of chest muscles.

The buzz of the café distracted my wayward thoughts. Pretty flowers hung from the ceiling in chalk-white potted plants. Lavender and wildflowers filled the space, and the music was a soft, chill vibe perfectly suited for the seaside. I shuffled in my seat, trying to get comfortable in a backless stone seat that could double as art. Yet as each minute ticked by, my behind felt more numb. Style over comfort seemed like the first choice here.

Outside the glass-fronted café, Blake paced. My attention wavered between eating mouthfuls of an Angus beef cheese-burger and watching him pacing the concrete sidewalk. His expression was grave. Hands regularly flew in the air as he likely pleaded his case to his boss and fiancé's father. From everything Blake said and didn't say about his boss, he sounded like a piece of chewed-out ass.

The server hovered over, her tartan apron wrapped around her tall frame. I shifted in my chair, diverting my attention from Blake toward her.

"I think this should go back under the heat lamps, don't you?" she asked accusingly. Her exotic accent matched the golden hue of her skin, brown eyes, and jet-black hair.

Momentarily she removed her focus off Blake, who'd been outside for nearly twenty minutes, and back toward me.

"No, thanks. He'll be coming in soon," I replied, hopeful.

She arched her eyebrow in disbelief. "If you say so."

"I do." I tossed her a fake smile, and she retreated not before momentarily gazing back at him over her shoulder.

Get back to work. Yes, he's God's gift to women, and no, he doesn't need you fawning all over him.

I sat there, surrounded by tourists, couples, and a few locals. Surprisingly, it was quite a nice place, except for the stuck-up servers. I realized, over the years, I'd become quite insular. Going to course after course occupied me. Whether it was floristry, yoga, Pilates, or trying my hand at the pottery wheel, I was always busy with something I loved. And when I'd taken the time to chill, it had always been in nature to a remote camp spot, never a café.

As I bit into my overpriced burger on a milk bun, I could see the appeal. At least I didn't have to cook. Or clean.

Reality had started to settle in. Alistair left me half his house, and Blake didn't seem at all annoyed by that. But surely, on some level, he'd be pissed. Blake didn't need the money. I did. Maybe he knew that. Anyone who could charter a helicopter last minute didn't give a flying fuck about the price of a cheeseburger. This was life-changing and undeserved. I don't know if I'd ever get over it, but I sure was going to try my hardest to restore it to its former glory.

I wasn't immune to using a power tool and certainly not afraid to get my hands dirty, but I'd pale compared to Blake. The man grew up around tools. But I doubted Blake had picked up a power tool since leaving Seaview and living his fancy new life. His hands, when they brushed mine, were smoother than silk. I swallowed, the feeling of his connection flooding straight in.

I cast my gaze outside, where Blake paced back and forth.

Blake's life was in New York now. So once we were done here, that's where he'd fly back to. I ignored the heavy feeling weighing against my chest. We had two weeks together. Then we'd sell it and move on. He'd forge on to create memories with his fiancé.

I let out a sigh.

Memories.

As each year passed, memories of my parents were slowly fading. And more often than not, I had to look through the family photo album just to remember their faces.

But selling meant I'd need a new home, not that that worried me. I always landed on my feet, and things seemed to work out just fine. So two weeks with Blake. I let out a strangled breath. Well, we would just get by for the sake of Al. I could push past the betrayal and how his hooded eyes lit a fire deep down low.

I could do that, couldn't I?

Absent for most of lunch, Blake had returned to a poke bowl with three cold eggs on top.

"How did it go?"

He swiped a hand through his hair. "Well, it wasn't great, Lil."

"Okay," I replied, waiting for him to elaborate.

"Let's talk about something else," he suggested, stabbing at his bowl of nutrient-dense food.

"Sure."

"Tell me about you, Lily. What have I missed out on in the last six years? Do you have a man in your life?"

"Didn't Al tell you I'm engaged?"

He lifted his head out of his poke bowl, eyes flaring. "What?"

Hurts, don't it?

"It's a joke, Blake. Relax." I studied him, the strain that crossed his face a moment ago easing.

Was he jealous? He was engaged and had no right.

"Right." He shoveled the salad into his mouth, and I couldn't help but watch his jaw move as he ate.

My attempt to lighten the mood had only darkened it as his silence stretched between us.

"There is no man." I sighed, breaking the swirling tension. "I've dated on and off since…" I let my sentence hang in the air, and he looked up.

"Since me?" His eyebrows pinched together in a question.

"Since you." My mind wandered momentarily back to the time when his hand trailed up the inside of my thigh, the feeling of my heart exploding out of my chest. The way he made me feel that no other man has made me feel since.

When I looked back up, his eyes were set on mine, a smirk appearing on the corner of his full lips.

Fuck, was he reading my mind?

"Tell me about them."

"Some were nice, some not so nice." Then came the verbal diarrhea, but I couldn't stop it. "My ex, Joshua, was probably my most serious. He asked me to move in with him."

A vein in his tick twitched.

"And why didn't you?"

"Don't know, didn't seem right."

"So you broke it off instead?"

"I did." *Why was I telling him all this?*

"When was that?"

"Over Christmas."

"Bet you're chomping at the bit then?" He flashed a wicked grin that lit the fire between my thighs.

"A girl doesn't need a man for that." *My skin flooded with hundreds of goose bumps.*

What was that… flirting?

I bit the inside of my cheek to stop myself from going any

further because, heck, it had been a while, and here was Blake, muscular, sexy… *No, I shook away the wayward thought.*

He ran a hand through his thick hair, his tongue swiping across his lower lip. "My, my Lil, now there's an image." The hum of the crowd disappeared as his stare chipped away my armor. Tension swirled between us, and it took everything inside me to speak first.

"An image an engaged man will never *ever* see," I fired back. Anger bloomed inside me like a tornado gathering speed. He had a woman waiting for him on the other side of the world, for fuck's sake.

"There are some images that cannot be erased," he said, returning to his poke bowl like he didn't just undress me with his eyes. "You know, Lil, I am sorry." My muscles tightened. My breathing suspended for a split second. "I'm sorry I left you in bed. Alone."

"Sorry?" I whispered out, barely audible.

"We were just kids, right?"

Kids? I nodded, words unable to form in my mouth.

"But I'm sorry. We shouldn't have… what I mean to say is I shouldn't have left and never called you." He folded his arms and leaned back into his chair.

Was he waiting for *me* to say something? *After six years, in a café where people hovered around us like flies, he was apologizing here and now?* For what exactly? Taking my precious V-card and leaving the next day? Or flying out and never speaking to his best friend ever again?

"Are you really trying to have this fucking conversation now? In a café? We are not doing this." I pushed out my chair in a rush. "I'll meet you in the truck."

Maybe I was trying to keep the peace because we were in such a public place. Maybe I needed to stay focused on the next two weeks. Or maybe, just maybe, I wouldn't admit to myself that he meant more to me than anyone since.

And that was that. The last six years of pent-up frustration, anger, and confusion were discounted in an apology that took less than a minute. Talk about a goddamn anticlimax.

We rode the entire way home in silence.

That apology, if that's what you call it, served him more than it did me. Truthfully, it was fucking pitiful, but I wasn't sure any apology so many years later could really be enough to rid me of my heartache.

We kept to ourselves that night—him in the house and me in my cottage. When tiredness finally came, I went to bed, where I tossed and turned in my wayward sleep, flickering between dreams and reality. Then, remembering how his full thick lips tasted on mine all those years ago, I willed myself to push him away and go to sleep.

Sleep must have come because I was awoken by howling wind and branches scratching against my bedroom wall. The sun had crept up, and I was thankful I got at least a handful of restful hours.

I went through my usual morning routine, except today, a feeling of uncertainty and fear settled in my stomach. Two emotions that were so foreign I forgot they existed.

I held my warm peppermint tea encased in my porcelain polka-dot cup. As I sat on my veranda with my fluffy blanket on my lap, I made a promise to myself. For the next two weeks, Blake and I could be friends. But that was where it ended. Sure, I could look and fantasize about what lay underneath that fitted shirt of his, but that's where I drew the line.

There would be nothing else between us.

Been there, done that.

He was engaged, happy as fuck, I think, and I wouldn't survive another Blake heartache.

9

BLAKE

U p before sunrise, and still, the band-aid apology I offered yesterday had been on my mind. Okay, so maybe the delivery could have been better. A hell of a lot better. But it was done, and we could move on. Work alongside one another for the next two weeks with no angst, awkward exchanges, or flirting. *Okay, well, maybe a little flirting. I wasn't Gandhi and fuck, she was gorgeous.*

My phone call to Robert was worse than I thought. The only other time I'd heard him that angry was when he'd torn shreds off his business partner, James Roche, for sleeping with someone underage. Not that he knew I'd overheard that conversation through the door.

I was his best moneymaker and halfway across the world. So, I understood his frustration. He even said he'd wire me what the house was worth just to get me back on the desk, managing the firm's investments. I nearly tripped over the pavement in front of me when he promised that.

I knew I was an asset. I was fucking good at my job. I'd done everything to be the best and sacrificed so much. But the fact he wanted to move Heaven and Earth to get me back was reason enough for me to stay. My old man was number one. And for some strange fucked-up reason I'm yet to figure out, he'd put that clause into his will, and I had to respect it.

Seaview was the last place I wanted to be, but being around Lily again was familiar. Still the same weird girl with the quirky style and flippant attitude to life, she knew how to get under my skin and set me alive with one glance. Feelings I tried my damn hardest to bury were returning way quicker than I wanted to admit. But I was here for just two weeks. Then I could return home. I just have to survive her for two weeks. *Two weeks.*

We organized the renovation straight up. She'd do inside, and I'd do outside. It was safer that way. Even though I had apologized, it was best to avoid each other whenever we could. She was becoming a temptation I couldn't afford to pursue.

Last night between work emails, I arranged a schedule for the renovation and handed her a copy of it this morning. Each day we had jobs we focused on to get it renovated in the allotted time frame.

When I returned from getting a morning coffee, she was sitting on the front step, sipping on her peppermint tea as she stared at it vacantly. I knew that look. She'd have the same vacant stare when I tutored her in math after school in the tree house. Okay, so maybe I intentionally gave her math problems that were even above her grade. There was something about her zoning out, then her punching me out of frustration. I'd do anything to feel her again.

It was mid-morning, and I still hadn't found the tools I needed. I squeezed between old tools, the lathe, and boxes throughout the garage in search of all the tools I needed to start the renovation. "Lil, do you know where Dad kept his saws?" I yelled.

She appeared in the doorway like pure sunshine. "That would be a firm no." She smiled, and it immediately pulled me out of my funk.

"I thought you'd know better than me." I raked a hand through my hair and noticed her stare linger. *Hmm, interesting.*

"I never came in here. By the way, does this fit into your schedule?" She grinned as she eyed me traversing the obstacles lying around the garage.

My attention strayed to her. It was difficult to peel my eyes away when she was wearing denim shorts that gripped her peach ass and a knotted T-shirt that showed her slim but not rail-thin waist.

"Had I known finding power tools would be this hard, I would have added on some extra time."

She let out a sigh. "When do things ever go to plan, Blake?"

"Ninety-nine percent of the time, they do! Better to plan than not. A plan is essential to stay on track and focused. Fumbling about left and right won't get you anywhere." *Maybe that's why you're still in the back cottage of Dad's place,* I wanted to say but refrained.

An odd expression flashed in her blue eyes. "But that all depends on your perspective."

Perspective? A shiny blade poked out from between two boxes. "Got it!" I let out an arrogant laugh and, with a hard yank, pulled it from its binds.

With a determined swagger, I made my way over to her. She crossed her arms over her chest at my smugness. Her stare lowered onto my body, and damn, it lit something inside me.

"Blake, you're bleeding!" By the shriek in her voice and the way she ran out the door, I knew it must be more than a paper cut.

Bleeding? I didn't feel any pain. I trailed the length of my arms. No blood there. Suddenly, a hot, burning sensation cornered my attention.

My gaze flitted down. Blood dripped down my shin, pooling into my white socks. "Fuck."

I set down the drop saw.

"Come in here." She appeared in the doorframe, returning with a bag of wipes and antiseptic.

"It's just a graze, Lil."

Okay, maybe slightly more than a graze but whatever.

"Just come in here. Why do men have to act all bloody tough…" Her voice trailed off, and I followed her into the kitchen, a slight limp to my stride.

She patted the barstool, and I sat on one while she pulled across the other. I lifted my leg onto the stool, the blood dripping directly onto the timber flooring.

"What's that?" I pointed to the brown glass bottle covered in dust she was holding.

"It's iodine."

"How old is that?" I snapped. "The bottle looks like it's from 1979."

"Probably is. Now quit it while I tend to this. Let's hope you don't need stitches."

"Well, some things never change," I muttered, remembering how she used to boss me around all the damn time. Whether it was on the basketball court, where she'd trash talk me out of a penalty shootout, or in the tree house, where she'd try and argue her way out of a math problem. I hadn't realized I had missed that until now.

She let out a groan as she stood at the side of my leg, assessing the streaking blood. Her scent, a cross between fresh linen and your favorite candy store, overwhelmed my senses. Strawberry blonde hair curled around her neck, where the same trio of freckles still ignited her skin. Suddenly, I wanted to reach out and touch her, but I gripped the barstool with cyclonic force instead.

A sting radiated up my leg, where she blotted the cut with the poisonous iodine. "Settle down." I gripped her hand, and she flinched at the connection. *I feel it too, baby.*

An unmistakable grin appeared on her face, and I wanted to wipe it away with an all-tongue kiss.

"You're enjoying this, aren't you?" I hissed out.

"No." She tilted her head to the side, but her grin spread further into her cheeks. "Well, maybe a little."

"I'm glad that hurting myself amuses you, Lily Stone."

She let out a low chuckle. "Lily Stone? Now I feel like I'm in trouble."

"So you should." My voice held low and gravelly. I pressed my hand in hers, and her eyes darted to mine before she released it from my grasp.

She fumbled, putting the lid on the bottle. "Well, we haven't even started, and the wolf of Wall Street is already bleeding."

I laughed. "The wolf of Wall Street?"

"Nah, what was I thinking? Leonardo streaks ahead of you in the cuteness department."

I rolled in my lips, my gaze hovering down to the curve of her ass wrapped in tight denim shorts with a thread of cotton resting on her thighs. *How I'd like to bend that perfect ass over and spread her legs right here, right now.* I gripped the kitchen counter and sucked in a sharp breath. *Get a fucking grip.*

Yes, Camille and I were diving into a marriage of convenience, but that didn't give me the right to play with Lil's heart again.

A crush, that's all. A familiar, gorgeous crush, that would be out of my life in two weeks. That's all Lily was. I couldn't dare let my feelings get in the way and hurt her all over again.

"That's fine, thank you." I lifted my leg off the barstool and stood. She'd managed in that short time to clean it up and bandage it. Actually, it looked much better. "Come on, we have a lot to get through in two weeks, and we haven't even started."

She thrust her hand on her hip, arching her back. I tried to ignore my dick twinging inside my briefs. "Hello? Look around. I've done a lot, actually."

I would look around if my eyes weren't drawn to you all the damn time.

Something squeezed inside my chest, finding its way to the base of my throat. Normally, I was able to manage billions of dollars without raising a sweat. But standing in front of me was a five-foot blonde bombshell, and I doubted my ability to remain in control around her for the next two weeks.

* * *

The day was going way too quickly. I sought comfort in retreating back to the garage after Lily cleaned me up. It was safer that way. Finding tools I hadn't held in my hands for ages brought back memories of building the cottage with Dad.

His chisel set that he'd owned as a kid, with the amber-yellow handles, rusted but still working as the day he got them. Or the lathe that hadn't been switched on in years. It was like an antique but powered up as if it was never off. The sound of the machine reminded me of the hours upon hours Dad had dedicated to turning wood, making the door cabinets or bench from local fallen trees that had dried in the nearby forest. Oaks, blackbutt, and red gums streaked with rich color created a warm, inviting home, one that wasn't the same with Dad gone.

It was late, maybe six or seven, when I went back inside. Dad's buffet, once full of old crockery and keepsakes now bare. As was his bookshelf filled with second-hand books from every genre you could imagine. Boxes stacked against it, taped up, and ready to go to the charity shop I'd organized.

"Hey," I eventually said after watching her for a moment too long.

"Hey, yourself." The tape gun screeched as she straddled

the box, running the tape down the seam, then smoothing it down with her hand.

How I'd love to see that view.

She had never been on top. I left before we could go any further. I was gentle when I took her virginity, restrained even. She was tight, wet, and perfect as I glided inside her. She lay on her back with me propped up on top of her. I remembered it like it was yesterday. How warm and perfect she felt around my cock inside her. It was intimate, warm, and nothing like I'd ever had since. When I entered her for the first time, her nails clawed my back, and I asked if she was okay, she willed me to continue, dragging her lips to mine in a heated kiss. And when we came together, it was then something changed inside me, and I knew I had to leave.

"You all right?" Her voice sliced through the trip down memory lane.

"Fine." I cleared my throat. "Shall I order takeout?"

I watched her hop off the box. "I can make us something," she offered. "Did you check the chicken coop for eggs today?"

"Now, that's something I haven't heard in a long time." I laughed, and a warm smile traversed her delicate face.

"Maybe not in Manhattan. I can make us some pasta if you want to check for me."

I scratched my head. "Why do you need an egg?"

"Egg, flour, and oil are the ingredients to make fresh pasta."

"You're making it from scratch?" I puffed out my cheeks in disbelief. *Was she serious?*

She stood, countering my shock with an equally confusing stare. "Yes, is that okay?" Without waiting for my reply, she added, "Grab a healthy bunch of basil and arugula so I can make a pesto sauce too while you're there."

Suddenly, her shoulders rounded as she hunched her back.

I came to her side. "What is it, Lil?"

"Oh, it's nothing." Her expression was pained.

"Lil, please, tell me what's going on in that beautiful brain of yours."

She blinked, then stilled herself. "It's just what I'd planned on making Al for dinner the day he died."

"Oh." Thoughts of getting takeout quickly vanished. I wanted her to be happy, and if she was making pasta from scratch when she was exhausted, then that was fine by me. "Which one is the basil?"

She giggled. And the same sound took me back to my last summer in Seaview.

Tonight was the night. I was hosting another epic party in my final year of senior school. It was only recently I'd started to host and let people come around to my place. I had Lily to thank for that. Chelsea Rose, the most popular girl in school and on-and-off again girlfriend, was draped across my lap, tongue down my throat.

But my eyes were opened and glued on Lily in her pretty red dress and black lace-up boots. Her long blonde hair in braids trailed down her exposed shoulders as she sat around the open fireplace with her friend, Jasmine, and my friends from school.

Then something Brennan said made her throw her head back in laughter. It only took a few minutes for Brennan to pull her away from the group and the snobby girls who sniggered at her outfit.

He handed her a beer from the keg, and I had this innate urgency to protect her. I started to make my way over to her when Chelsea wrapped her lips on mine again. Still kissing her, my eyes never left Lily.

The way she touched him, my blood fired. And at that moment, I wanted to be him. I wanted Lily's arms around me, her lips on mine. She was drunk. I could tell by the way her hands touched his shoulder for support, not anything else. He moved in quicker than a cobra, taking advantage of her. His hand fell to her waist, pulling her into him as he rested against the fence. She leaned in, her legs between his. Fuck, no!

In an instant, I pushed off Chelsea and began to run over to the far corner toward Lily. It was a slow-motion disaster. His hand found its way into her hair. Her face was close to his. Now, her hands rested on his chest.

No!

He kissed her. I was too fucking late.

"No, Bren—" Lily said, trying to stagger away from him.

"You know you want it, baby." Brennan grabbed her arm and pulled her into him.

My legs were heavy from my alcoholic-induced haze, but I only had a few steps left. Her first kiss would not be with him. It had to be with…

Whack.

My hand smashed into his jaw. "What the fuck, Blake?" He fell to the ground, clutching his mouth as blood started to pour from it, tinging the green grass red.

"Blake? What are you doing?" Lily screamed.

"You're a pussy, Blake." He spat, and blood sprayed on my new converse sneakers. I'd saved for months doing local paper rounds and cutting neighborhood lawns just so I could buy the same shoes everyone else had.

"She said no, bro," I yelled.

"Fuck off, Blake! We all know you got in on an academic scholarship. Look at this place. It's a dive. Like daddy, like son. You're going nowhere."

Rage burst like an overflowing dam. I came at him again and again, my fist pounding against his skin.

"Fuck, Blake. Stop, man." Hands gripped my chest, holding me back. I assumed it was Fabian and Rocky, my best friends. Problem was, the four of us were the best of friends.

"Jesus Christ, Blake, his face is ground meat," Fabian said.

"I don't give a flying fuck." I shook them off me and made my way to Lily.

I'd prove him wrong. I'd prove all of them fucking wrong.

* * *

"Blake?" Lily stared at me from Dad's kitchen. "Come on, let me give you a lesson in herbs and show you what basil is."

"Right." I still felt uneasy about the feelings coming up in the base of my spine and the pit of my belly.

I fell into step beside her. Her hands clasped around her elbows as she gripped her body from the gust of wind. The air was cool but still balmy compared to Manhattan. The sea breeze fleeced the maple trees of their leaves, leaving smooth branches in their place.

I slid into the chicken hutch and lifted out the eggs. Some were still warm, bringing back so many memories I tried to bury when I left.

"Basil has this oval-shaped leaf that smells rather like aniseed." She cut a large bunch and lifted it to my nose. *That's right, I remember now.*

"Smells good." Our eyes met for a moment, and something passed between us. My body flooded with warmth and heat. I had to drag my eyes away. Whatever was shifting, I had to put a stop to it, didn't I? I wasn't so sure anymore, but I quickly used the excuse of needing to get cleaned up to create some much-needed space between us.

I came in the shower with her blue eyes piercing mine, the image of her tongue swiping across her bottom lip, glistening from her saliva. I pumped my dick so hard I convulsed to her. Twenty minutes later, I entered the cottage, level-headed and less likely to come onto her now I had my release. But seeing her bare-faced and in shorts and a tee, my dick had a mind of its own.

I pushed past that and focused on the cottage she'd made her home. Being inside the house brought back memories of the endless days after school we spent nailing the shingles on the roof, painting the walls, and tiling the tiny bathroom. Upcycling materials we'd come by at the local dump—old vintage doors, an unused box of Moroccan tiles, skirtings, and even the beauty find, which were bifold kitchen windows. The same ones I'd stared out of now and into the garden.

"Come over her, Blake."

I peeled my eyes away from the art lining her wall and walked to where Lily stood in the kitchen. When our arms grazed, heat immediately trailed up my forearm to inside my chest. I turned to face her, and her clear cheeks glowed rose-pink.

Damn, we still had something.

"Here, put two fingers in the middle of the flour and create a well for the egg."

I did as she said following her pasta demonstration.

"Now watch out, I'm going to crack the egg in the center of the well."

She leaned over me, her heart-shaped face near mine. The dusting of freckles on her cheek and her natural pink-stained lips removed the air from my lungs.

"Now, with this hand, slowly incorporate the egg with the flour by making your circles bigger." She put her hand on mine and moved my two fingers into a circular motion. I imagined my finger circling her clit, watching her moan under my touch.

Fuck, this was like a scene out of Ghost, *minus the pottery wheel.*

"I like cooking," I said, my voice gravelly.

She tilted her face to meet mine, and I stared at her beneath hooded eyes, suddenly wanting to taste those lips again. She let out an audible gasp, and fuck, I was on fire, burning for her.

"I uh… I think you got it now." She removed her hand but not before her blush crept down along the side of her neck.

"I'm just going to, ah, m-make the pesto sauce," she stammered, pushing past toward the other end of the small kitchen, pulling out her pestle and mortar. "Tell me about Camille?"

And the fire is doused.

"Camille? Well, what do you want to know?" I asked, mixing the egg and flour so it was forming into a ball. "We met at a charity dinner last year that my firm, Jackson and Roche, put on. Robert, her dad, introduced us."

"Wow, don't go gushing, Casanova."

Why would I? It's a marriage of convenience. We're about to go head-on into a loveless marriage built on lies and deceit.

"What does she do for work?" Lily asked, genuinely interested in my life. The sentiment was refreshing, especially coming from an industry where it was every man for himself.

"She's a Manhattan socialite."

She raised an eyebrow. "That's a job?"

"Since the Kardashians made a living out of a sex tape, you bet."

Her laughter reverberated throughout the kitchen, settling in my chest.

Our eyes collided, and she was the first to look away. "She has a group of friends, and they go to regular charity lunches and dinners."

"Sounds like a keeper." Lily turned around and pounded away at the basil mixture in a mortar and pestle. Bruising it more than necessary in her relentless pounding, I wondered. *Was she jealous?*

"That sounded a little sarcastic, maybe a bit like jealousy?" She turned around in a rush, and I couldn't help but smirk.

"Jealousy?" Her voice shook loudly. "Are you out of your mind? What would I be jealous of? I have my own life, a full, rich life. She has nothing I want, and I mean nothing."

Ouch, that was a punch to the throat.

10

LILY

The last three days had been a whirlwind of packing and stacking boxes, finding moth balls in the strangest places, and sorting the throw-out pile from the boxes going to charity.

Blake arranged for a local charity to pick up Al's belongings instead of throwing them all out. I had to admit I was pleasantly surprised. In his line of work, I didn't think he'd care whatsoever if Al's stuff was dumped or repurposed.

I sat on my veranda, sipping my peppermint tea after my morning yoga. Blake had worked tirelessly outside, fixing shingles and reattaching fallen downpipes. And with the help of Moving Angels, I packed the inside up a lot quicker than I thought possible.

Blake had organized the help—saying it was perfectly within the rules. I wondered if he did it so I could be done with the inside of the house quicker and then be outside with him. In the last few days, I'd intentionally focused on being inside the house, trying to ignore him as much as possible. After all, that's what his well-laid-out plan suggested. But from a distance, I watched him work in faded jeans and a shirt that clung to his muscles, and when he came inside, I noticed my temperature rise, and my thighs ached for his touch.

It was in every look he cast my way, every long-winded stare and bone-melting smile. The air inside grew thick with lust and memories of what once was, and damn, it pained me to admit it, but Blake still had a hold on me as much as I tried denying it.

Then there was *that* dinner when I showed him how to make pasta, and the way his fingers moved in a circular motion with my hand guiding his. Since then, all I could do was picture his fingers circling inside me.

I took a large gulp of tea, and it seared the back of my throat.

Things have changed between us. And I was the first to admit that I liked it. Blake was back. The same man I spent a large part of my life with. The same man who protected yet hurt me to the bone.

I gazed into the house, the light already on. It had been on every single morning before I woke. Blake must be working. He always worked when he wasn't fixing the house. It's a life he wanted. A life of riches and never wanting for anything, except he didn't seem happy but just seemed to exist. I had this urge to want to show him my world where freedom knew no bounds and there was a life worth living outside four office walls. I knew it. I'd craved it since losing my parents and lived my life that way ever since.

The side gate creaked, and Blake walked in with his old surfboard tucked under his arm. His half-unzipped wetsuit hung around his waist, revealing his rolling torso that went down into a delicious V. *Jesus!* He'd filled out from the teenage boy I'd remembered. His chest was broad and his athletic body lean, not at all an office body.

I shrunk into the back of my wicker chair, watching him unglove out of his wetsuit by the outdoor shower. He rinsed off, letting the water come between him and his swim shorts, the dark line of hair trailing from his stomach down, down to his… *shit. Fuck.* My phone pierced the silence. Quickly, I leaned over the chair, nearly toppling over to pick the damn thing up.

"Hi, hello?" I whispered, but Blake's attention collided with mine as I gazed back up, half off my chair.

"Lil, you there?" the voice on the line called.

"Amber?"

"Yes, it's me. Why are you being so weird?"

"I'm not," I replied, my voice decibels higher than it ought to be. I watched as Blake flung the towel around his shoulders.

I couldn't seem to stop staring, nor could he. I may have dropped my blanket at that point too, revealing my bare thighs and matching camisole and shorts.

He raked a hand through his wet hair, his gaze electric.

"Okay. Dinner tonight, my place at eight. Jazzie will be there too."

"Uh-huh?" I mumbled. Blake's gaze disengaged from mine, then he turned and headed toward the house, every muscle in his shoulders and back rippling with each step. Each curve of his muscle spectacularly pooling a deep desire inside me.

"So? Is that a yes? They didn't teach me gibberish at law school."

Blake opened the screen door to the house. Looking over his shoulder, he tossed me a wink and a grin that sent blood shooting through my veins.

"Yes." I breathed. "I'll be there."

Old memories, that's all they were.

I took my sweet time this morning, consciously working slowly so I didn't have to go into the house and see him, especially after I eye fucked him in the shower. I picked my uniform of denim-holed-out jeans with dangling threads and a pale pink T-shirt with a red pocket that may or may not have been a size too small.

It was already eight-thirty, and I knew I should be up at the house helping him hammer away, but something held me back.

The corner easel held my half-finished painting. Its greens and blues mirrored that of the orchard and garden. I opened the chalk-white paint pot and quickly lay a few textured brush strokes against the cerulean blue skyline before my stomach started rumbling.

Fixing myself a bowl of yogurt with fresh raspberries from the garden, I topped it with a sprinkle of nut mixture and flipped open my laptop. The digital agency that regularly sent work my way had tasked me with three new marketing jobs. Looking at the contract, I could easily do this job in my sleep.

Hundreds of dollars a week came from it and over a thousand in a great week. But in the beginning, after my digital marketing degree, I'd taken anything from website design to media launches and horrendous social media marketing.

Now I could afford to be more choosy. Over the last few years, I'd built up my name online, and now corporations were approaching me directly rather than going through an agency. The fact that Al kept the rent so low was a bonus. I offered to pay him more in the weeks I could, but he just flat-out laughed.

I ate a mouthful of homemade yogurt as I clicked open on an unread email.

Lily,

This is Brennan. I'm sure you'd remember me.
I'm the Portfolio Manager at Chase Capital in Brisbane, and my marketing team ran your name past me for a PR job that needs doing ASAP—see the attached brief.

You up for the challenge?

Regards,
Brennan Jones
Chase Capital - Brisbane Office

I had to lift my jaw off the floor. Interesting timing.

The last recollection I had of Brennan was Blake colliding with his face after he'd tried to kiss me. My body shivered as I read the attachment. I could do the required job, and the remuneration was amazing.

I should take it, considering I hadn't taken a job in a while, and my savings were running low. Then there was the reality that I'd have to find a new home, which required savings for a deposit. Yeah, so I needed the money.

Quickly, I tapped out a response, agreeing to the job. Here's hoping his marketing team would be my contact rather than directly dealing with Brennan's asshole face.

A head appeared around the window, followed by a body of sin.

"What are you doing, Lil? Shouldn't we be renovating?" He smiled warmly, and it hit me between the feels.

"Sorry, I had to get back to a few job prospects I didn't get back to last night. That's how I make a living."

"How's that exactly?"

"Online marketing jobs, copywriting, public relations, anything really. Agencies employ me."

"Sounds sporadic." He cast his gaze toward the half-finished artwork I had propped up on a wooden easel.

"Wow, that's amazing. Is that…" He turned from the artwork to the orchard.

"Yes, that's the orchard. Many mornings I sit outside here and just paint. With the sun rising, there's simply nothing better."

"I remember." He slid through the doorway, past the kitchen, and into the living room, where I sat on my loveseat.

"I hadn't noticed before, but it's rather eclectic in here. You have lots of stuff for a tiny house."

"I enjoy being surrounded by different things. It's cozy."

He ran his finger along the shelf where various pottery vases and dishes sat along with glazed bowls with Japanese inscriptions and floral overlays adorning the area. My book-shelf was littered with romance novels—some old, some new—but no other genre. Crammed up against those were unglazed dinner plates, currently curing before I returned to fire them in the community kiln.

And taking up half of my bedroom, sticking outside the doorframe, was my pre-loved Pilates machine, a discarded trea-sure I found on my walk along millionaire's row, where houses grew from the ground up almost overnight. A faulty spring was the only thing preventing the mechanism from working. Al helped me source one and replace it to be brand spanking new. Once I completed my course, I started running private lessons with clients here in the cottage. A great little money earner, but I slowed it down once I started floristry.

Shit!

I'd completely forgotten about floristry. I had missed two lessons since Al passed.

"I'll just be a sec." While Blake wandered throughout the studio, I quickly emailed my teacher, apologizing and assuring her I'd be there this weekend.

"It most definitely is cozy." Blake hung in the entrance to my bedroom, leaning against the doorframe. Just then, I noticed the swirling of butterflies in my belly.

"What's that in the corner?" he asked, and even though I knew what he was talking about, I got up and stood beside him in the doorframe.

"That's my Pilates machine."

"And what on earth are you doing with that?"

"I'm a qualified Pilates Instructor."

He tilted his head to the side. "So let me get this straight. You're a qualified Pilates Instructor. You obviously know how to do pottery because it's everywhere. You are currently learning floristry. Help me out here, what else am I missing?"

I smiled, but I was sure it didn't reach my eyes. He could mock me all he wanted, but I was blissfully happy. And no one could take that away from me. That was a choice.

"Hmm, part-time camper, qualified short-order cook, and I was thinking about scuba diving next."

"You're joking?"

"Not at all."

"Having limited funds… doesn't that scare you?"

I shot up an accusatory eyebrow, and he lowered his gaze. I decided to keep my new job offer to myself, especially considering I'd taken it with Brennan, the same man Al said he'd leave the house to should Blake leave within two weeks.

"Well, you're living in Dad's back cottage… one would assume…" He stepped inside my bedroom, and my heart rate spiked. *Okay, get it together, girl.* I hung in the doorframe, creating a safe but small space between us.

"Blake, I pick up odd jobs online. I don't plan too far ahead. History has clearly shown not once but three times to me that nothing lasts forever." I fixed my steely gaze on him.

Did you just compare your parents' death and Al's death to losing Blake?

Strain etched across his eyes.

"I can do whatever I want with my time. That freedom, it's priceless."

He came to stand opposite me in the doorframe with his arms crossed and let out a sigh but remained silent. Something swirled between us—frustration, uncertainty—something unfinished. His manly scent was drenched in his loose tee where his biceps gave rise to hundreds of goose bumps, and his workers' pants clung to his thighs.

He lowered his eyes to my lips and automatically, I sucked in my lower lip, inhaling a sharp lungful of air. When his gaze met mine, it was dripping with burning desire, and the air turned thick as heat laced my chest.

No.

What the fuck?

I squeezed past him.

His eyes bore into my back as I walked toward the kitchen. The air in the room was stifling. *I didn't imagine this. Did I?* He was engaged, yet the pull we had on one another was intensifying. It was there in the final few months before he left, and it was damn sure back. Except this time, I had to fight it with every fiber of my being, and so did he. I would not be the other woman. *Ever.*

11

BLAKE

F*uck!* What was wrong with me? I wanted to kiss her all over, rake my tongue over the freckles at the base of her neck, and finish between her thighs. The way those bright blues stared back at me, they were equally vulnerable and fierce. I knew my apology meant nothing. She wouldn't have rehashed our past even if it did.

"History has clearly shown not once but three times to me that nothing lasts forever."

Fuck.

What we had before, I was beginning to feel it was more than I gave it credit for. A night of sex and taking my best friend's virginity wasn't just *one* night, after all. We had history —a deep friendship built on trust and loyalty. That's probably why I snuck out without her waking. If I'd waited for her to wake and had to look into those beautifully framed indigo blues, I don't know if I would have got on that flight.

But I did. I firmly pushed her into the recesses of my mind —hidden—and flew across the other side of the world because I was driven as fuck. I was headstrong to get the hell out of a small town and the furthest away from a guy and his family who were determined to ruin my life because busting open Brennan's nose came at a price.

I'd broken his nose in three places, and Brennan's dad—a noteworthy physician—had threatened legal action. Then there was no ignoring the fact that Brennan's dad had connections, and he was determined to ruin me at any cost. So disappearing on a plane to New York seemed the right thing to do—get away from the mess I'd created in the last few months and ensure Dad kept the house while also doing him proud by putting my good grades to good use.

But it was comments like that that made me wonder if I let the best thing in my life get away.

I slapped my leg. My fingers tingled up my hand from the force. Around the front of the house was where I found my hammer. Intentionally avoiding walking through the house to get to the front, I went the long way. I didn't trust myself, especially around those tiny shorts and blissful eyes. Then there was the fact I was engaged. *Fuck.*

The back door creaked open, and after a while, I heard her moving about inside, occasionally humming to herself through the living room window.

Over the next half hour, we worked our separate parts of the house, me on the outside, nailing in new boards to replace the hollowed-out termite boards, and her inside, actively avoiding me.

Her humming turned into the occasional lyric, and from outside, it sounded like fucking rainbows and sunshine.

"Lil, can you help me for a while?" I asked, the words tumbling out of my mouth before I could stop them.

Dangerous territory, Blake.

"Be right there." Suddenly, she appeared out front and jumped down the two stone steps I'd restored. Wearing a floral headband and going makeup free, her bare face caught the light—velvety smooth skin that made me want to reach out and run the back of my hand down it.

Camille.

You're engaged to goddamn Camille.

But even reminding myself of that fact seemed trivial. After all, it was just paperwork. She had already made that abundantly clear. Her riding a stranger in our bed set that into motion. But strangely, I wasn't upset or lovesick. I was fucking bitter. That competitive edge always reared its head, and there it was. I wanted to kill the fucker in my bed, but that had nothing to do with her.

Love, I'd never experienced it. *Why would I?* When I saw my father crash and burn after his wife fucked around on him, I swore I'd never let myself be in the same situation he found himself in. Being vulnerable did strange things to men.

But then, everything I'd worked so hard to achieve was within reach. Yet strangely, it didn't feel quite right. The marriage was for show, a mere convenience, a step to getting ahead in a company where I was already streaking ahead. Being part of the Jackson family would propel me into another league. The family name was prestigious in Manhattan and etched in tradition and money. Knowing Robert Jackson, he'd make me sign an ironclad prenup. But if shit went south, that still meant millions. He hinted at it in his office. And I'd be lying if I hadn't thought about it since then. I was only human.

Lily bent down and picked up the hammer, my eyes connecting with her pert ass as her entire body jerked with each contact she made with the wall. Petite and willing, she didn't let that stop her from hammering the hell out of the nail. Her go-get attitude was so refreshing and sincere and not laced with a predetermined motive or agenda that I was so used to in my line of work. The more time I spent with her, the more I wondered if she, all those years ago, was the closest thing to love there was.

The thought jolted me.

"I'm guessing this is what you need me for?" she said, banging the nail into the board with a force that looked at odds with her slim frame.

"Jesus, okay, Popeye, settle down." I sided up behind her and quickly grabbed the hammer as her arm flew back in preparation for a full swing. My hand tightened around hers, and she stilled, her body against mine. The heat off her back warmed my chest.

I tilted my chin onto the crown of her head, where the rose and gardenia flower scent of her hair filled my nostrils.

My thumb grazed hers. "Let me show you." My voice held gravelly low.

"How to use a hammer?" She whipped around, but with nowhere to go, she fell back against the wall, a whisper away from me.

I stepped closer and rested one hand on the wall beside her head, and the other still joined with hers on the hammer. The wind stirred the leaves as they rustled on the ground next to us.

Ocean blues stared back at me as I saw her throat bobbing up and down. My gaze flitted across her jaw, leveling on her rose mouth. She was so close I could almost taste her. Instinctively I leaned closer, but before I could go any further, she'd wrestled the hammer from my grip and slid out from underneath my hand.

Fuck.

She turned over her shoulder to face me. "What are you doing, Blake?" Flustered, she pushed her bangs out of her eyes.

I leaned against the wall for support. *What am I doing?*

When I didn't reply, she thrust her hand on her hip. "Blake, you're engaged, and this…" she pointed her finger back and forth between us, "… this is just…" Wanting her to define what this was, I let her finish.

"This? You and me. We are so done." Her voice was level,

but underneath that, there was a hint of a tremble I simply couldn't ignore.

"It doesn't feel done."

She took a step back.

"The moment you left me in the middle of the night to board that plane, we were done. Then every day after that, you ignored my phone calls and emails. We were done."

"Lil, I know I fucked up back then. I had something to prove to myself and to all the Brennans out there who thought I was nothing. I wasn't good enough for you back then. I was nothing."

"You were my best friend. My first love! My first everything! Then you went and forgot I even existed. "

"I never forgot about you. I've thought about you every damn day, Lily."

She shook her head, angst plastering her pretty features.

"Were you thinking of me when you put a ring on another girl's finger? Or what about when you and Camille were basically fucking on the street outside your building?"

"What are you talking about?"

"I was in New York. I came to see you. Right before I got out of the cab, I saw you two dry-humping like a bunch of teenagers."

I remembered that night. Camille was drunk, high, and all over me. I heard a cab driver yell, "Get a room." I held her upright and turned to see a cab idling on the street outside my building.

Lily was in New York? "Wait, that was you?" I was in shock. I raked a hand through my hair and down my neck. "Why didn't you—"

"I realized you moved on, Blake, and what would be the purpose of talking at that point?"

"Lil, just because I'm engaged doesn't mean I've moved on… it doesn't mean I've ever gotten over you."

She threw her hands up to the sky. "Oh, my God! Who are you, Blake Carter? You are engaged to another woman. You can't say this shit!"

I'm a guy spearing headfirst into a loveless marriage. The guy who chose wealth and power instead of taking care of my father, and the jerk who left the only person who really mattered in my life.

"I think it's best if I stick to the inside. I'm going to paint the bedrooms."

"Maybe that's for the best," I replied

She frowned, then walked toward the house.

Good one, Einstein. I smashed the nail into the wall, hammering it like Thor, God of Thunder.

I was losing it. What was I doing here? Being here in the house I grew up in was sending me into a goddamn head spin.

I let out a grunt. Maybe hearing Camille's voice would help remind me of our impending nuptials. Get my head back in the game I clearly needed.

The door slammed, and I knew she was inside. I took out my phone and dialed Camille's number, noting that the only people in my quick redial were her and her dad, Robert. *Fuck, when had my life become that detached?*

"Camille?" The background was so loud Dad's neighbors could likely hear it punch out of my smartphone.

"Blakey?" God, I hated when she called me that.

"Where are you?" I asked, my voice elevated.

"Geez! Would you just wait a minute," she snapped.

I shook my head. *What was I getting myself into?*

"I'm at the Met. The fundraiser with Adriano is on."

"Oh, right." *Another one?* They were all the same to me.

"How's Australia going? Spot a crocodile yet?"

Fuck me.

"It's slow. I'm doing up Dad's house, trying to restore it before we sell it."

"We?"

"He left half to me and half to my old neighbor, Lily." Just saying her name to Camille felt wrong. Not because I had feelings for Camille but because I felt this need to protect Lily from her.

"Lily, the love of your life, Lily?"

Suddenly, I felt disorientated. "What did you say?"

"God, every time you drank, you spoke about her. Your eyes lit up like firecrackers."

I muttered something even I couldn't understand.

"Well, if it makes you feel less guilty for fucking her, Jordan's waiting for me at his apartment after this," she replied flatly.

"First of all, I'm not fucking anyone, that's your MO. Let me be clear here, I don't give a damn who you fuck. What I do care about is discretion."

"Oh, of course, that's all you care about."

I kicked the tree stump, and a shooting pain shot up my toe to my chin. "Camille," I snapped, on the verge of completely losing my shit.

"Fine, we have an understanding," she bit out.

"Good, now please your father and get your monthly trust fund allowance."

"If anyone knows about pleasing Daddy, it's you, Blake. You're never home. I had to find a way to take care of my needs."

"Well, someone's got to keep you accustomed to your way of living. And what kind of excuse was that, anyway? You're supposed to socialize, get a job. I don't know, do anything but fuck around so blatantly. At least have some self-respect."

"I have self-respect." Her tone turned ice-cold and full of venom. "And I do have a job. It's making you and my father look good. Now I have to go, hubby. I'm bidding on this China tea set… all for charity, of course."

"Camille, we are not finished," I growled out, barely controlling my anger.

Silence rang down the line. "Camille?" I yelled. "Fuck!" I looked up to find a couple walking by. They looked vaguely familiar. They turned to me, and the lady's mouth half opened as her husband shook his head.

"Sorry." I waved.

My phone pinged, and I released my thunderous grip, flicking my wrist so the screen was visible.

Robert Jackson's name was highlighted in my messages.

Robert Jackson: *Where's the fund report? I needed it yesterday, Blake.*

"Double fuck."

I quickly punched out a reply.

Me: *Getting it to you in an hour.*

Three dots hovered as he typed a reply immediately.

Robert Jackson: *Hurry the fuck up.*

Like Dad, like daughter. Both pains in the ass.

I trudged up the steps and flung open the screen door. Hastily, I pulled out my laptop and immediately set to work.

Half an hour had passed, and I was still pounding the keyboard when Lily strolled inside to fetch another can of paint. She eyed me sideways, then returned to the bedroom without saying a goddamn word.

So what if my gaze fell to her ass? Sue me. I was just looking while my fiancé fucked the town.

I hit send on the email to Robert with the report he was waiting on.

Lily's melodic voice echoed through the house. It was a cross between Enya and Florence and the Machine, majestically calm, the sound pulling me away from my slump.

When she emerged, the Alabaster white paint found in the garage was smeared on her nose and in her strawberry-blonde hair. *Damn, why did she have to look so adorable?*

"I'm calling it a day," she said, barely acknowledging me.

"Already?"

"I have dinner plans." Her eyes flicked up to meet mine as she tied her shoelace on the barstool. I wondered what it would feel like for that leg to be wrapped around my waist. She did fucking Pilates. She'd be more flexible than a rubber band. The thought sent a rush of blood to my dick.

Wait, dinner plans? Does that mean she had a date?

"What kind of dinner plans? Who are you having dinner with?"

She narrowed her eyes. "A friend."

"That's it? A friend? Is this a friend with benefits?"

"Blake, you have no right to ask that. And don't think for a second I'm giving you an answer. I'm leaving. I'll see you in the morning."

"Fine," I snapped, jealousy igniting my blood to damn near flammable. "Be ready bright and early. We have loads to do."

"Yes, boss." She sighed.

"I like the sound of that." I grinned.

"Such a flirt." She lowered her leg, and her lips slightly parted.

"And I think you love it…"

She walked toward the door, and my breath held in my throat.

Look back. Turn around, gorgeous.

"See you tomorrow, Blake."

I exhaled in a rush. There was hope yet.

12

LILY

Amber's apartment was only a block away, so I walked. For years she shared with Jazzie until Jazzie met her Prince Charming a few months ago. An unlikely match, and one that took her off to New York to be with Kit, her happily ever after.

Jazzie, here for the funeral, was leaving again tomorrow, flying out to start her own photo exhibition in a well-known gallery in New York. She was the missing piece to our trio, and I didn't realize how much I missed her until I saw her again at Al's funeral.

Two flights of stairs later, I rapped my knuckles against the pine door.

"It's open," Amber said in a normal voice. The apartment was small enough, and the walls were paper thin. So much so that she'd soon gotten to know her neighbors' weekly Wednesday night sex romp. *Hump Day really was Hump Day in this case.* Luckily for Amber, she only had to suffer all two minutes of it before it was over. Still, she'd put up with the fake moans and shoebox apartment for the never-ending ocean view and sea breezes.

"Hey!" Amber's brown hair fell loose around her shoulders. She set down her glass of red and reared up to sandwich me in a hug. Jazzie appeared from the black and white checkered bathroom to get in on the Lily sandwich.

"Okay! Hello!" I hugged them back with a squeeze, then let go, needing some space.

"Amber, get the woman a glass. She looks like she needs one." Jazzie took me in.

I'd changed into a casual slip-dress and paired it with Doc Martens. "Ah, I'm offended!" I mocked. The truth was, exhaustion oozed from my pores and was no doubt evident on my weary face. "Thanks." I took the glass from Amber.

She flopped back on the sofa beside a packed cardboard box.

"What's that for?" I gestured toward it with my wine in hand.

"Jazzie's just packing up the last of her things to take back to New York."

"Kit wanted to arrange an international moving company." She laughed. "Can you believe that?" But love bloomed on her face from his over-the-top kind gesture.

"How is Kit?" I asked. It was nearing two months since he'd flown us to New York to see Jazzie.

"He's perfect. Really perfect." She couldn't help but blush from ear to ear.

"And New York?" I added.

"I'm ashamed to say I love it."

"Why are you ashamed?" Amber inquired, tossing back her wine.

"I know we are family and Seaview is my home. I've left all that behind."

"Ah, well, that's reasonable." I shrugged. Truth was, I did miss my friend so much, but if she was happy, then so was I.

She threw a decorative cushion at me from where she sat on the armchair. It landed on my arm, nearly spilling my wine.

"Watch it!" I squealed.

"I ordered pizza." Amber smiled, topping up my glass, then pouring herself another.

"Oh, food. I could eat the ass out of a donkey." One or two pieces were definitely not going to cut it tonight. I salivated at the thought of devouring an entire pizza after today's renovation workout.

"So what's happening with you, Lil? Has Blake gone back to New York? You know you're crap at returning phone calls," Amber remarked.

"Yes, sorry, a lot has happened." I steadied myself for the onslaught. "Alistair left me half the house."

"Shut up." Jazzie flicked away her red hair and leaned forward, green eyes like saucers.

Amber set down her glass. "You're serious?"

I nodded, ingesting a big gulp of wine. The dark rich flavors slid down my throat, leaving me wanting more. "There are conditions."

"Oh, this sounds right up my alley. What are they?" Amber straightened, the lawyer in her standing to attention.

"Blake has to stay in Seaview and renovate the house for two weeks with me. If he doesn't, he forfeits his share, which he'd do, if it weren't for the next condition."

"Two weeks together?"

"Shh, Jazzie!" Amber put her arm out in protest. "What's the next condition?"

"If he leaves before the two weeks are up, the entire estate goes to Brennan Jones."

Jazzie's eyes enlarged the size of hula-hoops. "What the fuck?"

I let out a sigh. "I know."

"Why would he do that?" Jazzie asked.

"Wait, back up. Who's Brennan Jones and why does that name sound familiar?" Amber added.

"He's the guy Blake punched out in the last year of school." I couldn't help the slow smile spreading on my face. And the way Blake was so protective of me when Brennan tried to take advantage.

"No, I wouldn't know him from there. I didn't know you both then. Hmm…" She rubbed her left temple. "Anyway, continue. I'm sure it will come to me."

"Brennan once upon a time was Blake's friend, along with Rocky and Fabian. The four of them were inseparable until that party," I said.

"Gosh, that was a good party. All the rich snotty Grammar kids with their designer shoes and short skirts. Oh, the fun we had, Lil. But then Brennan decided to hit on you, and that's when Blake charged in, fists first," Jazzie added.

"Gosh, I wish I knew you guys back then." Amber let out a chuckle.

"We were a handful. We took nada from no one." Jazzie winked.

"Still don't," Amber added, and we all erupted into laughter.

The melodic chime of the doorbell sounded. "That's the pizza. Stop right there! I want to hear the rest of the story."

"Right-o." I topped up my wine and welcomed the blissful haze spreading throughout me.

Jazzie cast her eyes over me. "You know, there was this undeniable chemistry between you two back then. And I'm not talking about Brennan, although he was cute too. It almost took Blake seeing you with another guy to act on his feelings for you. Feelings he'd obviously had for a very long time."

"Maybe. I don't know. We always had *something*. I felt it, and that night I think I saw it come out of him for the first time. At that moment, we definitely were more than friends.

We weren't just flirting anymore at afternoon math classes or shooting hoops, where he'd always manage to touch me more and more. He actually punched Brennan out. He said he did it because I was drunk and didn't know what I was getting myself into. But, of course, I thought it was way more than that."

"Okay, I'm back." Amber placed three large pizzas on the wooden coffee table, flipping the lids and handing us napkins. "Sorry, no plates, don't want to wash up when I have emails looming. What did I miss?"

The cheese and ham smell of the pizza filled the apartment.

"I'm just so confused," I said, sliding out a piece of cheese pizza.

"Well, there is still something there. I sensed it in the kitchen after the wake, and I'd only just met the guy," Amber replied. "But you told me how upset you were after he left. I don't want you going back to that, hun."

"Me too," I whispered. I recalled the night I lost my virginity.

I woke up at his friend, Fabian's mansion alone and felt slightly sore from the previous night when Blake and I took the next step. Unlike everyone else, we were sober and fully aware of what we were doing. Walking downstairs to find empty cups strewn on the plush knit pile and hung-over half-naked bodies of fellow Knights Grammar students, but no Blake anywhere. The walk of shame was brutal.

The sad part was that it wasn't even the worst part. On the bus ride home, I thought the worst. What if he was sick? Or what if something happened to Al?

But it was none of those things. He'd just up and left me like I didn't matter.

"So, how's Blake about it all?" Jazzie asked.

"Angry. First, I thought it was because he would be away

from his fiancé, Camille, and work, but now I think it's more about work and leaving the house to Brennan if he quits."

"He's engaged?" Amber asked.

"Yes. I forgot that part. To the daughter of the hedge fund owner, Robert Jackson."

"Really?" Jazzie's face screwed up.

"What?"

"Camille Jackson, Blake is engaged to Camille Jackson?"

I nodded. "Do you know her?"

"Yes," she replied quietly.

I snapped, growing more impatient by the second. "Well, go on, speak!"

"She was at a charity dinner in Noho that Kit and I went to last month. Blake wasn't with her. I'd obviously tell you if he was."

"And?" *Was it getting hot in here all of a sudden?*

"Anyway, Kit's bandmate, Jamie, spotted her snorting blow with a server just before he went down on her in the coatroom."

I spat out my wine.

"Sounds like quite the catch." Amber half-laughed.

I fidgeted with my bangs.

"What is it, Lily?" Amber asked, scooping a pillow to her chest.

"I overheard a conversation I probably shouldn't have today with him and Camille."

"Oh, who needs Gogglebox? When the three of us get together, there's too much to talk about," Jazzie added with a smirk.

"Yeah, I know, right? It doesn't sound like the first time, either. I heard Blake say, 'Let me be clear here. I don't give a damn who you fuck. What I do care about is discretion.'"

Amber covered her mouth with both hands in shock at what she'd just heard. "So it's all a sham?"

"I think it might be. It didn't sound like a couple about to tie the knot and spend a happy ever after."

"And Blake's on board. Why?" Jazzie asked.

"Her dad is a zillionaire," Amber added, taking a piece of pizza between her fingers.

"I don't know. That doesn't sound like Blake," I added. "He was always determined to be wealthy, but all on his own. Like he had to prove it to himself."

Amber widened her eyes. "Let's google her," she said with a mouth full of pizza.

"Amber, really?" I toyed with my bangs, the ends now oily from the pizza.

"You know you want to." Amber flipped up the screen on her laptop without waiting for a reply.

Yeah, who was I kidding? I wanted to know everything about the woman who thought cheating on Blake Carter was a good idea.

"If all this was true, then… shit."

"What is it now, Lily?" Jazzie asked.

"Well, he may or may not have tried to kiss me before I overheard this phone call today."

"Well, for fuck's sake, why didn't you start with that?" Jazzie threw her hands up.

I shook my head, regretting the opportunity that had gone by. "Because it doesn't matter."

"Your first love tries to kiss you, and you don't think we'd want to know that?" Amber steeled her eyes away from the laptop and glared at me.

"He's going back to New York in just over a week."

"That's just geography," Amber said, typing on her keyboard.

"He's engaged," I countered.

"In a fake engagement," Amber argued.

"And he hurt me beyond words."

"Literally, the guy didn't talk to her from the night he took her virginity until the funeral," Jazzie added.

"Thanks for the reminder, Jazzie." I let out an audible sigh. "Listen, I've had enough Blake talk for one night. If we don't eat this pizza, it's going to get cold and stodgy."

Thin, stunning, and tall. *Perfect.* That was Camille Jackson and all her images that stared back at me from the laptop.

"Yeah, she's pretty hot." We scrolled through the images of Camille that came up on Google images. The more I saw, the more depressing it became.

"If you're into plastic. My vagina has more wrinkles than her," Amber added, and we all burst into laughter.

I took a few bites, hoping to fill my mouth with food so I didn't have to talk anymore. My skin tingled. Hope sprung like a flower in bloom. *If the marriage was indeed a sham, then would he go through with it? And if he didn't, what did that mean for us?*

If there still was an *us.*

We got off the topic of Blake and onto Amber. She spoke about her extensive workload and never-ending cases at a law firm she worked for. I don't know. Maybe I was wired differently. But ever since losing the ones I loved, I couldn't imagine anything worse than being tied to a job and not seeing beyond the inside of an office all day.

I let Jazzie and Amber's chatter fade into the background. I needed to clear my head. I had to get lost, go into the wilderness and get back to my roots. Every time I did that, I came back refreshed and ready to take on the world.

Munching on my fifth piece of pizza, I decided tomorrow I'd do just that. I would work all day on the renovation, then grab my backpack and tent and bus it to the national park. I'd find myself a beautiful secluded spot near the century-old caves and just be with nature.

* * *

"Have a safe trip back, Jazzie." Amber hugged her goodbye.

"Don't be sad, Lil. I'll be back before you know it," Jazzie said, pulling me in for a hug. It felt warm and safe, and I didn't want to let my best friend go. She waited for me to pull back first, and after a beat, I did, already missing her.

"Call me when you land, and Lily…" Amber turned to me, "… you, keep your damn phone on. I want to know what happens with Blake!" Amber said, waving her lanky finger in my face.

I rolled my eyes. "Nothing's going to happen." But even I started doubting my own words.

"Just be careful. I don't want to see you heartbroken again."

"I'm older now. Some would argue wiser." I smiled.

"Not many." Amber grinned.

"Shut up, bitch!" She let out a chuckle and opened the front door.

"You right to walk, hun?" Amber asked. "I can call you an Uber?"

I shook my head. "I'm fine."

"I don't know why I ask sometimes." She released me from our hug goodbye.

I walked beside Jazzie as she carefully carried her box of keepsakes down the stairs.

I stopped suddenly as we reached the sidewalk. Waiting out front of Amber's apartment block was an idling limousine. "Whoa. No Uber for you then."

She smiled. "No. Kit wouldn't allow it. I have to admit, it is nice, though… being spoiled. Perhaps you should try it sometime."

I frowned. "What's that supposed to mean?"

"Money isn't the enemy, Lil."

"I never said it was."

"I see how you look at Amber when she speaks about work.

The long hours she does. Don't hold it against people if they're driven just because it may not be your thing." She placed her hand on my shoulder, and we embraced.

I watched the limousine disappear down the quiet street, leaving me alone with my thoughts as I walked the short block home.

Fumbling at the back gate, I tripped over a stone that lined the pathway. I gathered myself and walked toward the cottage. *What time was it?* Deliciously, my mind felt hazy and light from the merlot at dinner.

I jammed the key into the locked door, shouldering it open. I'd forgotten to leave a light on. Not unusual for me to forget, but tonight after a few wines, I stumbled around for the light switch. "Dammit!" My leg bumped into something, and blistering pain throbbed up my shin toward my knee.

Momentarily, I put aside the pain and found the light switch. The cottage was freezing! The slip dress I wore was now no warmer than a leaf. I slipped down my dress over my hips and to the floor, throwing it onto the couch. *Where did I leave my pajamas?*

"Whoa."

I whipped my head around, and Blake rounded the corner. Disheveled sandy-brown hair hung around his face dusting the tops of his ears. Dressed in nothing but gray tracksuit pants and a bare chest, he looked fine. Actually, he looked better than fine. *Damn.*

"Blake!" I stood in my Victoria's Secret bra and underwear, glued to the floor.

Our stares collided, and sparks arrowed between us. No longer was I freezing. Instead, I was a volcano of heat and lava at the point of combustion if I stared at his wall of muscles any longer. Quickly, I yanked my dress hanging over the couch in a lame attempt to try and cover up.

"Sorry," he mouthed but made zero attempts to stop staring.

"What the hell! A bit of privacy." Slowly and possibly a bit reluctantly, he turned around.

I poked my head through the dress and slipped it over my hips. My cheeks warmed as my thighs pressed together, and I ran my fingers through my bangs. "Okay, you can turn around." I exhaled. "What are you doing here, Blake?"

"I heard a loud bang." I watched his Adam's apple bob up and down as his eyes trained on mine.

"Well, I'm fine. You can see that I'm perfectly fine."

"I can see that." He scanned me from head to toe, then back up to my face. My thighs clenched tighter as an ache pulled between them.

"You can't look at me like that," I snapped. "Not anymore." Although, it was what I wanted more than anything. Desire pooled into my core, but my anger anchored it to a standstill.

"Why can't I look at you like that? You're a beautiful woman, Lily Stone."

"You left me, Blake. When I was at my most vulnerable." Blood heated my cheeks like a blasting furnace. The alcohol kicked in just at the right time, giving me the courage I needed. "We had this magical night. You held me, then one thing led to another, and you took my virginity. But then you left without saying goodbye. Who does that? I thought you cared about me. I thought you even loved me. I was so wrong. You fucking disappeared, never speaking to me again. Who the fuck does that, Blake?" By that point, I was yelling as rage flooded my veins.

"I told you I was sorry," he muttered.

"At a café? That was not an apology. You apologized for your own conscience. That wasn't from the heart, and it wasn't real. The word *sorry* doesn't make up for the last six years."

He stepped in closer, and I could feel warmth radiate from his skin. *Was it possible to want to kiss him and kill him at the same time?*

"You're drunk," he whispered.

"Yes, I am. So what?" I hissed out, then steadied myself against the wall from his intimidating closeness. "You know what, Mr. Self-Righteous, I need to be alone. I can't be around you, Blake. I'm taking tomorrow off. I'm going hiking in the national park."

"You can't do that." His dark eyes lingered over my mouth before meeting my gaze.

I took a step back. "I can, and I will. Those conditions only applied to you leaving, not me. I can't be around you. I just need a break. I'll see you in twenty-four hours."

"Lil, come on," he pleaded, but I couldn't relent. I was fuming.

"You with your fancy job and everything so put together." I was flapping my hands now uncontrollably, unfazed by how ridiculous I looked. "I know you're not put together.

I overheard your conversation with your supposed fiancé." I watch his eyebrows knit together in a frown. "You were outside. I was in the house, and the window was wide open."

He narrowed his eyes. "And?"

"Why would you commit to a life with someone who doesn't love you? She clearly doesn't love you, and now I'm starting to think you don't love her."

"That's none of your business," he roared, but I wasn't afraid. Blake didn't scare me.

"You're right. It's not." I stalked closer toward him, and he held my gaze, fury and desire in his stare. "And this…" Lowering the corner of my dress, I showed the hint of my bra. "You'll never get to see it again. So don't ever look at me that way." I shoved his chest hard, and he stepped back. "I'll see you Saturday." I slammed the door in his face.

13

BLAKE

All day. All fucking day, I hammered away. Thinking about what Lily had said. *The nerve.* She had the nerve to say that about me? When all along, she was the one who wasn't together. Camille made a mockery of what we were. She'd cemented that after fucking a random on our feather and down duvet, ass-up on an alternate cock.

I was in too deep with both father and daughter, chained by ironclad arrangements with a soon-to-be-wife and the career of my dreams. I had wanted both. But being in bed with Camille and her father lacked the luster it once had. But as the day went on, my need to see Lily grew stronger. So strong that it was all I could damn well think about.

My foot pressed the pedal so it hit the floor. The beat-up pickup roared with a new lease on life as it thundered down the highway, whizzing past cars like that were stationary.

I had to tell her the truth. Then we could go our separate ways. She could be blissful in her utopia of random pursuits, and I could go back to New York in a week's time and forget small-town Seaview. Forget Lily. Being in New York, I'm sure things would make sense again.

I curled my thick fingers around the steering wheel, hoping my Thor-like grip would make me arrive faster.

The highway exit came into view. Behind it, the faint hue of lilac and salmon slashed the evening skyline. I took the exit and sped along the quiet streets, anxious to see her. The street lights flickered on at the same time my phone vibrated.

Robert's name flashed on the screen. *Fuck.* I slammed my hand on the steering wheel. The force sent a sharp pain up my forearm. He didn't care that I'd just buried my father. That was done. I was just supposed to get back to work, right?

He worked around the clock and expected anyone who worked for him to do the same. Otherwise, you wouldn't work there. They think sending an ostentatious bouquet of flowers that hardly fit in the doorframe negated that. Yesterday, the smell was so bad I'd thrown them straight into the dumpster.

But my dad just died. Surely, an inch of breathing room wouldn't hurt?

Fuck it!

I had better things to do.

A calm washed over me as I sent the call to my voicemail.

I followed the signs to the national park. It would just be a quick visit to tell her the truth and get it off my chest. Then we could both move on. The guilt I carried would disappear, and my life would return to normal. *Wouldn't it?* I raked my hand through my hair, uncertain about my perfect plan.

I hadn't the faintest clue where she'd be or how to find her. And the last thing I wanted to do was to call her. Based on how bright her cheeks burned with anger last night, she'd hang up on me or, worse, tell me to go home. And I couldn't do that. Not until I apologized.

A handful of cars were parked on a carpet of leaves as I pulled into the entrance. Lily had stubbornly caught the bus when she could have asked for a lift. Did she really hate me that much? I sucked in a breath. The thought stung like a swarm of wasps.

For some reason, I couldn't let go of her resentment toward me. She'd trespassed on my mind and wouldn't leave. The more I tried to push her away, the more I thought about her. Knowing she hated me was like pouring acid down my throat. *But what else did I expect?* The best of friends, we'd always been so close.

Waiting for her to slide open that picket fence gate and greet me with that smile was the best part of my day. Or when I got to tutor her for math and secretly studied every curve of her heart-shaped face and the swell of her breasts through her tunic. Time had almost stood still.

I locked the pickup truck and started walking down the trail, my Northface jacket shielding me from the arctic chill in the air. Each step took me further away from my truck and deeper into the forest. Different shades of green flooded my view. Tiered rainforest plants, native birds, and rustling trees overtook my senses—a welcome distraction from the car horns and bustling Manhattan streets. I sucked in a lungful of clean air.

I'd missed that.

Missed the surf.

Missed *her*.

I *really* missed Lily. I hadn't realized how much until now.

Leaves crunched underfoot as a fire flickered up ahead just off the pathway. I hoped it was her, especially now that the limited daylight had disappeared and my only light source was my phone's flashlight.

"Hi, Lily?" I peppered through the trees, hoping she heard me.

"Nah, man, no Lily here." A group of guys in their late teens curled their heads around the fire.

"I wish there was!" a sleazy voice added.

A vein ticked in my neck. Dammit. She wasn't safe out here on her own. I had to find her.

"Are there any more campsites nearby?"

"Yeah, keep going down the track," the guy with the tattoos on his face said.

"Helpful," I muttered.

She wasn't fearful of camping in the middle of nowhere by herself. She really didn't fear anything. I loved that about her, but if those guys saw a gorgeous woman camping on her own. *Fuck, how could she put herself in this situation?* Heat scaled my back as my steps became more urgent.

Camille would freak. Let's be real. Camille wouldn't even camp. Her idea of slumming it was in my apartment on the Upper East Side. It was a matchbox compared to the mansion she was raised in and the holiday houses she frequented in Monte Carlo and St. Barts.

Why was I even comparing the two of them?

Nestled between two huge canopies of palms, a faint light flickered up ahead.

"Lil?" I yelled out as I approached the vaguely familiar-looking tent.

Nothing.

Fuck.

"Lil?" I repeated. This time I was only a few yards from the tent.

A faint ruffling sounded from inside the tent. A second later, the zipper lowered.

Dressed in leopard-print leggings and a carrot-colored turtleneck only she could pull off, Lily stepped out.

"What the hell are you doing here, Blake?" She was all five-foot-nothing but full of bravado. "And how on earth did you find me?" Her brows shot to the moon in surprise.

"You told me last night when you were drunk. You told me where you'd be."

Her eyes darted from the fire and back to me. Her fingers gripped her hips at right angles, her nostrils flaring with anger.

"Just wait, Lil, please." If her body language was anything to go by, I had about two minutes before she sent me packing back to the pickup.

My chest heaved at the thought of leaving her alone. "I just came to say what I need to say. Then I'll leave."

"Fine," she snapped, releasing a hand to rake her bangs over her eyes.

The fire crackled and snapped, its shadow dancing against the tree trunks. Nerves swirled inside my stomach. *What the fuck? Since when did I get nervous?*

I pushed them aside. I couldn't wait any longer to say what I came here to say.

Inhaling sharply, I stepped close. "I'm so sorry for what I did to you, Lily."

"You've already apologized," she deadpanned.

"No, I didn't. Not properly anyway."

She rolled her eyes. "Well, fuck, you don't say."

I held up my hands, white flagging her. "Okay, I admit, it was a shit apology. But I am truly sorry for pretending you didn't exist. I was lying to myself for all those years. The truth is I should have never shut you out."

"It was nothing," Lily said, echoing her previous sentiments, but her voice softened as her gaze fell to the fire.

But it wasn't. It was everything.

You were everything.

Another step over the rocks and fallen leaves.

I needed her eyes on mine again.

Desire filled my chest, knocking against my heart with a sledgehammer.

"You don't believe that, do you?"

Step.

Standing still, she swallowed down the lump in her throat. I circled her hips, my thumbs pressing into her hip bone. She didn't move, but I pulled her close so the gap between us disappeared. I tilted her head as my hand feathered her jaw.

"I don't know what to believe, Blake."

Her eyes shone in the moonlight, and tears glazed her ocean blues. She was the most beautiful woman who existed.

Thick desire lined my throat as tingling warmth filled my veins.

I wanted this. She wanted this. Without thinking, I leaned down, my mouth crashing on hers. She tasted of apples, berries, and *Lily*. Her smooth, velvety lips were everything I remembered. She groaned in my mouth, and damn if that sound didn't just ignite my dick. My arm snaked around her hips, digging into her ass and pulling her into my thickness. Her slender body pressed into mine, her hands in my hair, her touch feverish.

Our tongues desperately hunted one another like the teenagers we once were. Her hands fell to the nape of my neck, pulling me close as she rubbed up against me. I groaned out at the feeling, warmth spreading up my spine.

"Fuck, I want you, Lil." My voice held thick and low. Her hooded eyes stared back at me, thirsty with desire. This time it would be different. We weren't kids anymore. "Come with me." I held her cheek in my hand as she nodded in my grasp.

I lowered the two-person tent zipper and bundled in, pulling her by the hand close behind me. A bed of blankets and a sleeping bag lined the tent floor as she zipped it up behind me.

"I never left you, Blake," she confessed, and something in my heart exploded.

The vulnerability in her eyes was like the deepest part of the ocean.

I shuffled out of my jacket as I pulled her onto my lap. I stared at her longingly, wanting to please her to no end.

Laying her down, I clawed at her skin-tight leggings, peeling them down her smooth thighs until she tossed them aside. She then flung her sweater over her head, revealing her bra.

I stood and admired her. *Did she know how gorgeous she was?* Her tits, natural and large, spilled over her lace cups. Curves, smooth skin, freckles damn near everywhere, and I remembered every square inch.

She was perfect, and she was mine.

Fuck me.

"Ms. Stone, well, aren't you fucking something else."

She dug her teeth into her lower lip. "Well, you don't get to have all the fun." She widened her ocean eyes. "Undress, Blake."

I let out a slow, sexy smile. "No. We have all the time in the world, and I intend to savor every last drop of you first."

She inhaled sharply at my dirty words.

I breathed out, trailing the inside of her thigh with hot wet kisses. My mouth landed on her cotton underwear, and I thrashed my tongue along the cotton of her slit. She gasped and lifted her hips to my mouth, craving more.

"Baby, you're already so wet for me."

She moaned out at the connection. "Touch me, Blake."

Fuck, she was heroin on a stick—*addictive*. I unclipped her bra and pushed down her underwear, revealing her delicious dark blonde strip of pubic hair to the most delicious cunt.

Crushing my lips on hers, she opened for me, tongue thrashing against mine in desperation. I trailed one finger between her legs as our kiss grew more heated. I slid inside her folds with one thick finger. *Fuck.* She was dripping for me.

Alternating between her clit and wet pussy, I went to work, wanting to please her like no other. The sound of her desire smacking against my fingers made my erection hang like lead above her.

"Oh, God," she groaned out with a hiss. "Blake." She shut her eyes as an orgasm built.

"Not yet, baby," I said, removing my hands and taking them to my lips.

She stared at me wide-eyed and panting with need, and I licked off her desire with my tongue.

Unable to wait any longer, I leaned down between her thighs, spreading her wide.

Fuck, I'd dreamed about eating her out so many times I'd lost count. We had skipped that step and went straight to sex that night.

Licking between her folds, I swiped my tongue in and out, lavishing every inch of her. I shivered in pleasure. This was my thing. And fuck I was a selfish prick because I enjoyed it as much as her. I slid my tongue across her aching clit, then deep inside her. Flicking and massaging her deep inside, her orgasm was swift and explosive.

"Blake!" she cried out. I circled her harder with my tongue and pulled another orgasm from her as she fell apart around me.

I let out a throaty groan, imagining how she'd feel around my cock. Damn, I was so close just watching her respond to my touch and unravel around me.

Eventually, she opened her eyes. "That was…" She paused, trying to catch her breath. "Unbelievable."

I licked the corners of my mouth as my hands ached with a need to touch her.

As though sensing my need, she purred. "Too many clothes, Blake." Her warm breath was a direct message to my groin.

I snaked my hand down my back and yanked my T-shirt over my shoulders. She pulled it off as she wiggled underneath me, wrapping her legs around my hips.

"Off," she ordered as she unbuttoned my jeans.

My dick throbbed. I liked dominant Lily.

I'm not going to think about how many lovers she's had since me. I don't want to end up in jail for murder.

In a second, I legged my jeans and boxer briefs off, springing my thick cock free.

Her eyes hooded as she took me in. *Yeah, baby, that's all because of you.* She raked her teeth across her bottom lip.

Outside, the flame licked and crackled, lighting her up like the goddess she was underneath me.

"I need you inside me, Blake."

Damn, those words were like honey, and carnal desire shot through my veins.

I reached for my wallet in my pant pocket and pulled out a condom.

She grabbed it from me and tore the corner with her mouth. "Let me."

Damn, that was hot.

"Not so innocent anymore."

She let out a smirk, and with curiosity, I watched her guide it down my tip, all the way down my shaft. Her eyes lifted to mine, and I sucked in a breath, already playing out the fantasy in my head.

She laid back down, and I laid on top of her, resting my elbow on either side of her head to prop myself up. I kissed her with untamed desire as I gently slid my tip inside her entrance. I lowered myself into her and hissed out at the connection.

Sweet and tight, she gripped me as I inched my way inside her tight walls.

"Fuck, Lil."

We moved together slowly at first. Then more frantic. Lily rocked her head back, revealing her neck and the smatter of freckles just below. I sucked her neck, breathy hot kisses trailing her collarbone, the intensity almost overwhelming. We bucked together, her hand finding my hair as she balled it in a fist. Her other hand clawed at my ass, her nails digging in and sending my pumps fast and furious. She clenched again around me, knowing it drove me wild, and I hammered into her harder.

Her moans were louder, her muscles tighter. She was close. I thrust into her harder and deeper, her hips angled higher as I hit her G-spot.

"Fuck, Blake," she cried out, throwing her head back as she clenched and uncoiled around me.

Watching her unravel tipped me over the edge. "Lil," I said through clenched teeth. My eyes rolled into the back of my head as I found my release.

Sweat beaded along my back as I dipped my forehead to hers. Our rapid breathing slowly returned to normal after a few minutes.

There wasn't anywhere in the world I'd rather be but here. And that was too fucking scary to admit, even to myself. I rolled off her and laid down on my side, staring at the tent's roof.

"Well, that was so much better the second time around." She rolled onto her side and placed her hand on my chest.

I laughed. "Well, in my defense, the first time, you were this gentle innocent thing. Not now."

Her laugh echoed in the stillness outside.

Tiredness came over me, and I pulled her closer so her face was against my chest. We were two naked bodies bathed in warmth, lying underneath a canopy of stars, with the crackling of the fire.

Her lips grazed mine as I fell into a dreamless sleep.

14

LILY

They say never repeat your past mistakes, but what if Blake wasn't a mistake?

What if he was my everything?

Waking up in the crook of his corded arm, I wondered how long he laid awake, watching me sleep. It wasn't long until our naked bodies tangled again. With duvet covers flung to the side and me straddling him, enjoying the view of his deliciously carved body and thick legs, I came twice this morning then we dozed again.

I woke first, admiring his full lips and his sharp jaw dotted with stubble. I let myself imagine what a life with Blake would be like. Only for a moment, but I quickly stopped myself. I didn't know what this was or where it was going.

What happened last night and this morning beat the hell out of me. But happiness poured from me like honey dripping into a teacup.

Between packing up the tent, driving back in the truck to the house, and continuing with the renovations this morning, I was exhausted.

It was just before noon, and the sun was directly over the house, beating down its fall heat.

Blake toed out of his boots, setting them neatly beside the front door. *I ought to try it, considering how messy my cottage floors were.* "Hey, beautiful."

"Hey, yourself," I said, unable to hide the blush creeping on my cheeks. The image of him gazing up at me from between my thighs had been on a loop all morning. Goose bumps shot down my arms, making me all warm and tingly again.

Fuck, when was sex ever this good?

Never ever with my handful of boyfriends did it even compare to this.

"Hungry?" I asked. He must be after all the hammering going on outside.

"Always," he replied, with half-lidded eye and a wicked tone. He leaped over the few boxes in front of me and scooped me up off the floor, tossing me over his shoulder like I was a toothpick.

"Hey!" I slapped his back.

He slapped my ass. Then his thumb found my skin and that ticklish spot on my hip bone.

"You're insatiable." I grabbed onto his thick head of hair for support and curled it beneath my fingers. "But I'm actually hungry! For *food,*" I emphasized, and he let out a groan. "I'll take a platter of orgasms later, though."

He squeezed my ass. "And I'd be happy to provide those." Gently, he lowered me to the ground, and my lips brushed against his. I had to force myself not to tear his clothes off here and now.

"And to think you could have had this all this time." I winked.

He opened his mouth to speak but then stopped. He stared at me but wasn't focusing on me. It was as though his mind was swirling around with thoughts, ones I so desperately wanted to tap into.

I cleared my throat, unable to handle the tension. "Come, I'll make us some sandwiches."

"I'll need more than a sandwich for what I want to do to you later."

And just like that, Blake was back. His dirty words, I could hear all day long like my favorite song on repeat. Desire pooled in my belly, sending an ache between my legs. "You haven't tried my sandwiches." I ran my tongue across my lip, and his eyes burned with desire.

Fuck, I could have him again and again. Right here in Al's home. Okay, maybe not right here. Luckily, my bedroom was less than a hundred yards away. Fluttery sensations swirled inside my chest and stomach as the anticipation for the afternoon lay ahead.

"I'll be back." I trudged off to my cottage, feeling his heated gaze trace my steps out the door.

The sun streamed into the kitchen windows of the cottage as I hummed a familiar tune. The birds sang, just like they had this morning in the national park. A harmony of bellbirds and kookaburras echoed around the burned-out campfire as dawn broke through the canopy of trees, filtering fingers of light through the tent. Beads of morning dew fell upon us as we rattled the tent. I laughed out loud at the thought.

I looked down at my handy work. Homemade bread buns overflowing with pulled pork, camembert cheese, and slaw made from the preserved crop of cabbages in the garden, all served on two seafoam green plates I'd made in pottery class.

"Okay, let's just make something clear. When you say sandwiches, I pictured cheese and ham. But this, Lil…" he licked his fingers, "… this is no cheese and ham."

I smiled slowly, pleased with myself. "So my sandwiches are impressive, Mr. Fancy Pants?"

He quirked a thick eyebrow. "Your culinary skills aren't the only impressive thing."

I let out a laugh, and he inhaled a sharp breath.

"When did you learn how to cook?"

I shrugged. "I don't know. I guess when I moved out of Aunt Josie's. I got sick of two-minute noodles, so I decided to pick up some second-hand cookbooks at the charity bin and went from there."

"No wonder Dad loved having you here. But baking your own bread, who has the time for that?"

"Bread is super easy. Most things are, if you have the time and the produce. You should have seen the garden in spring. It was bursting. I couldn't keep up! It's so satisfying growing then picking your own apples for chutney or chilies for relishes and growing red onions then making caramelized onion jam."

He looked at me sideways. "I love my job, Lil, but damn, I don't speak about it with the same level of passion you do. Your passion for all things is both contagious and confusing."

I tilted my head, mimicking him. "It just fills my bucket."

"Fills your bucket?"

I smiled. "Brings me joy."

"Money brings me joy," he was quick to reply.

Jazzie's little speech about money flooded in. *"Money is not the enemy, Lil. Don't hold it against people if they're driven, just because it may not be your thing."*

Curiosity trumped judgment so I was keen to find out more. "Money comes and goes, Blake, but tell me, why do you think money brings you joy?"

He shrugged. "Maybe because Dad was a carpenter by trade and going to Knights Grammar, I saw the other side of the coin… how the other families lived. They had everything they ever wanted growing up, but I had to save my ass off to get the latest sneakers or pack of basketball cards. Now, I have the freedom to buy whatever I want."

I leaned forward over the counter. "Yes, but do you have the freedom to buy it when you want it?"

He exhaled. "No, not like you, at least. You just take a mini-holiday when the thought takes you there. I haven't taken a break since arriving in New York." He raked a hand through his hair. "This, right here, is my first break from work. And it took my Dad dying to get it."

"That's sad, Blake."

"It's life. Anyone who takes a break in my line of work is diving headfirst off the Empire State Building. It's career suicide. You might think it's sad, but it's just reality. You should get a whiff sometimes." He softened the blow from his words with a heartfelt smile. Yet, underneath that was a truth I pushed away.

"I can't say I understand managing other people's money, but you're not saving lives, are you?"

He laughed a deep laugh. "No, Lil, I'm not saving lives."

"Didn't think so." I twisted my lips.

The afternoon flew by. The rain settled in, and so did Blake, moving inside to help me paint the last bedroom. We'd made some serious progress in the last week. Blake had removed all the weathered panels and replaced them with newer ones while also fixing the rusted downpipes with new ones. The front steps had a new handrail, and the tired front garden was cleared and ready for planting.

Inside, I'd been super busy packing up the entire house with the hired help. We left the vintage sofa in place and some old pieces that Al had made—beautifully carved furniture that would help to style the home. Blake even suggested I take the furniture when we sell the house. He said Al would have wanted me to have it. The sentiment moved me.

The painting had started and was nearly finished. A fresh white coat of paint had replaced the beige walls making the space more open and bright.

"I'm going to miss this house," he admitted.

"Me too." I glided the roller back and forth in the paint tray. "You know, when I was packing the photo albums, a photo of us in the tree house slipped out."

"That place was my second home." Blake smiled broadly at the memory.

"Mine too, especially when we relocated from the kitchen counter to the tree house for math tutoring."

"Ah, very fond memories there." He lowered his stare the same way he used to when it was just him and me alone in the confined space of the tree house. Heat snaked its way down my belly, wrapping around my thighs. I swallowed the cement in my throat.

"Is that why you suggested we move to the tree house? I knew you were checking me out!"

He laughed. "I wanted you all to myself."

"You dirty math tutor, you." I winked. And with one arm, he lifted me and kissed me hard on the mouth. I kissed him back, and for a moment, I'd forgotten I was holding the paint roller.

I felt something drip down my thigh, and reluctantly, I peeled my mouth from his.

Blake looked at the alabaster white paint streaming down my denim overalls. "Oh shit, sorry!"

I laughed. "Don't be, they're just clothes. I'd take washing to have that kiss again any day."

He shook his head, surprised by me. "Nothing fazes you. Does it?"

"Not really."

"No, that's not true." He widened his eyes.

"What?"

"You don't remember? The spray can? I got you so good, you were bitchy as fuck for a solid week after that!"

"That's because you spray-painted my hair with bright blue paint!"

"Fuck, that made me laugh so hard."

"Oh, I remember." I groaned, thrusting a hand on my hip for effect.

"You're getting flustered about it right now!" He laughed.

"I am not!" I snapped.

"You are, and it's adorable. Say, if I peppered you with kisses, starting at your neck and working my way down…" He paused, and I watched as his Adam's apple bobbed up and down in his throat. "Would that take your mind off it?"

He stood with broad shoulders and half-hooded eyes. The air in the room swirled with years of chemistry and insatiable desire, swiping the air from my lungs.

Just create some space, Lil.

"That would help, yes, but perhaps after we finish up here?"

He twisted his lips into a smile. "Sounds like a plan, little one."

He picked up his roller and effortlessly glided the roller with long thick strokes, covering the wall with ease. The muscles in his back rippled under his shirt, his broad shoulders tapering into his slim waist.

A thought came to mind as I watched him paint. "What was it that you painted on the ladder leading up to the tree house?"

He stopped painting, his arms hanging slack at his sides. "You forgot?"

Okay, so perhaps I knew exactly what it said, but I needed to know if it was that important that he remembered too.

"Lil' and Blake. Always and forever mates."

"That's right." I turned around so he couldn't see my face. The pain of him leaving me was too much to bear. "Each step had a word on it leading up to the tree house too."

"Sure did."

"We have had so many fun times." I glanced over my shoulder to find Blake smiling wide.

"Memories to last an eternity," he sighed. Taking a deep breath, he continued rolling as silence descended upon us.

Eventually, he spoke, "How many times did we have dinner up there together?"

"Loads. Luckily, we skipped it the night the storm pushed the tree onto our beloved tree house, smashing it in two."

"That wasn't damn luck! I had to drag you back down the ladder in the pelting rain."

I giggled. "Ah, it was just a bit of lighting and rain."

"That broke the tree house in two!" he said in a strangled cry.

I laughed, and he shook his head. His gaze turned inward. "You're crazy, Lil."

I wrinkled my nose. "That's what you love about me."

Wrong choice of words, Lil. I glanced up at him, his expression was unreadable. *Fuck!*

"I, um, didn't mean… that's not…" I threaded my bangs with my fingers. "Why did you tutor me in math anyway? Was that something Aunt Josie and Al concocted? To get my grades up?" *Damn, it was all I could think of asking.*

"Probably. Fuck. I loved watching you squirm at the simplest equations." He laughed, his face illuminating.

"You sicko. You probably made them extra hard just so you could torment me."

"Watching you focus was so fascinating. It was weird. There was something about the smell of the wood, your washed hair, and being so close to you in that tiny tree house. That's when things changed for me. I didn't look at you like this blonde girl who played basketball and climbed trees. I noticed your long legs, sin-worthy curves, and that smile… it was the best part of my day." He cleared his throat. "You were so easygoing it was contagious."

I rolled the same patch of wall, paralyzed by his honesty. Unable to turn and face him for fear of completely breaking down, I eventually added, "We had something, Blake."

He exhaled. "I know." A thickness formed in my throat as he admitted his feelings, but it was too little too late now.

"You know what else I found?" I asked, trying to break the heaviness that fell between us.

"What's that?"

"I found Brennan's book. You know, the signed one you stole from school."

"Oh shit, no, you didn't." His green eyes glowed brightly.

"Oh, but I did." I flashed him a wicked grin, and his eyes widened.

"That night after I punched him out, Al grounded me for what felt like forever. But that precious book, I had to do everything in my power to get it."

"Why was it so important again?"

"Bill Gates signed it, and the nerd wanted to build his own Microsoft empire. Anyway, we fished it out of his room. Fabian and me. Like literally fished it in the middle of the night with Dad's fishing rod. I swear the guy was never the same again. He always thought it was me but could never prove it. Even got his daddy to speak to Al, asking him to fess up, but I buried that book."

I nodded in agreement. "I know you did. I found it in an old shoebox in the second bedroom under the bed!"

He laughed, and the weightless sound flooded me with warmth.

"Fuck, I don't even remember putting it there."

I picked a fresh patch of wall to paint. "You know, oddly, Brennan contacted me last week."

He set his roller in the tray, and I felt him arrowing holes into my back. "Why the fuck would he do that? Have you stayed in touch with him over the years?"

His tone made me turn. Redness lined the side of his neck. *Was he jealous?*

"No, but even if we did, why would it matter to you?"

"Tell me you never slept with him, Lil, after that night when he tried to kiss you." His jaw clenched, and all of a sudden, my calmness turned to annoyance.

"What the hell, Blake? You left me, remember? Not the other way around. It doesn't matter who I slept with… you weren't here!"

His hands balled to his sides, and his nostril flared. He looked like, at any moment, he would commit first-degree murder if I didn't step in.

I closed my eyes. When I opened them again, I took a steady breath. "No, I didn't sleep with him. He contacted me for work, all right?"

His eyes turned up, looking heavenward.

"Where does he work?" he asked as his fists released.

"He's a hedge fund manager in Brisbane, ironically the same as you."

He flicked his gaze upward. "No, not the same as me."

"I didn't mean it—"

"Why does he want to work with you?"

"Apparently, there's some bad PR about to hit the news, and he wants me to flood the media with good news stories."

He sheathed his teeth. "That guy was always trouble and a pain in my ass."

"Why, because he tried hitting on me?" I let out a shaky laugh.

"Not just because he hit on you. But because he tried to get you drunk to take advantage of you. There's so much more. You need to stay the fuck away from him, Lily."

I could tell he was growing more irate, so I needed to steer the conversation away from Brennan and me quickly.

"Do you think Brennan knows about the deal with the house and how Al left it to him if you didn't follow through on your two weeks in Seaview?"

"No. He couldn't, possibly. I don't even know why Dad did that. It's just so random. It's not like Dad to not tell me about something as strange as that."

"Maybe he was trying to teach you a lesson?"

He pursed his perfect lips. "Like what? Sharpen my carpentry skills because I haven't used them since I was eighteen?"

I shrugged. "Maybe. Or maybe he thinks Brennan might just be your lesson."

"How's that?"

"He's everything you wanted. He had it all, and you were jealous. Now it's your turn to have it all. But do you?"

He laughed. *He actually laughed.* "Honestly, Lil, sometimes…"

I widened my eyes as my shoulders curled into my chest. "You know, I think I'm done for today," I muttered, setting my brush in the paint tray.

"Of course. I'll just finish this room off, and I'll join you."

I didn't bother putting up a fight. It would have been false anyway. I craved the man, even if he didn't want what I wanted. I wanted him to be with me tonight and the next and the next until he had to leave. I'd be hurt all over again, but I'd deal with that then. This was now, and I lived for the now.

Although, I wondered if I could deal with losing him all over again.

"Just let yourself in." I trudged toward the door.

"Hey, wait a minute, beautiful" Thick fingers wrapped around my wrist and pulled me into his firm chest. He kissed me gently, and I melted into his arms. Without hesitation, I opened for him, and his tongue desperately traced my teeth. I peeled up onto the tips of my toes, wanting to feel the force of his lips as they burned on mine.

Desire pooled everywhere as nerves stood on their ends. "Hurry," I whispered.

15

BLAKE

Lost in her beautiful blues, I traced my hand down her cheek. Every fiber in my body ached for her. I dug my finger into her hips, dragging her down harder and matching her rhythm as she rode me. Perfect tits bounced, and swollen rose-colored nipples begged me to take them again in my mouth.

"Ah, Blake," she moaned as she slammed down on me, clenching so deliciously on my shaft.

Fuck me.

Each time she lifted her hips, the sensitive part of my tip nearly spilled over in ecstasy.

She leaned over, grabbing the bedsheet beside my head and fisting it between her fingers. I licked and swiped my tongue over her erect bud, sucking and biting it until she moaned. The sound made my dick want to explode.

How were we this compatible?

"Kiss me." I grabbed her chin and dragged it down on my face. I needed to taste her.

She did as I asked and her kiss, moist and breathless, sent every nerve ending into the stratosphere. She peeled her lips from mine, gripping my hand as she quickened her pace. I wrapped my fingers around hers and squeezed. I watched her with awe as she arched her back and unraveled around me.

"Oh, my God," she breathed out, her sex clenching around my cock.

The sensation tipped me over the edge as heat slashed across my chest. "Lil," I groaned, my eyes rolling back into my head as I lost all control.

Panting, she fell on top of me. Her featherlight weight was warm and dewy as she pressed into my chest.

It felt like home.

She felt like home.

I reached beside my thigh and pulled the blanket over us, and our breathing slowly returned to normal.

After a few minutes, she moved her leg to the side to climb off me.

"Can I stay?" I tilted her head up, her tired eyes finding mine.

"Mm-hmm," she mumbled sleepily.

I ran my fingers through her hair and down her spine as her arms fell across my chest. Our breaths fell into sync as we rested in silence. Her face nuzzled into the base of my neck, her warm breath and heartbeat, two sensations I suddenly couldn't live without. I didn't want to be anywhere else.

Lily drew longer, deeper breaths, one after the next, and I lowered my gaze to her. Her eyes were closed, "Lil?" I whispered, but her eyes remained shut.

Thick black lashes dusted across her rosy cheeks as I lay watching her sleep. Time stood still. And suddenly, the thought of leaving her again ignited a fresh wound inside my chest, one I wasn't sure I could get past again.

* * *

The days that followed were equal parts joy and relaxation, which was the last thing you expected when undergoing an intense renovation in such a short amount of time. But with Lil, there weren't any problems, only solutions.

We finished both coats of paint on the bedrooms, laid the new carpet, and had a contractor install a new shower door. The last thing needed was a vanity, and instead of buying one off the shelf, Lily suggested I use my carpentry skills and make one. I thought she was crazy given our deadlines, but here I was, choosing a piece of stacked timber in the corner of the garage where long slabs of wood had been curing since the storm years ago.

Typically, insurance would clean up the mess the storm caused, but because we couldn't afford that, we had to clean it up ourselves. Dad had milled the fallen tree and stored them in the garage ever since.

Nothing gave me more pleasure than the earthy smell of raw timber. I'd forgotten just how much I enjoyed the pastime of woodworking. With the summer heat at our backs, the garage felt like a furnace, but that didn't stop us. We turned wood into furniture legs and detailed cupboard doors and made chopping boards and bowls. Usually, by dinner, my tank top would be covered in shavings of wood. Lily would laugh at the state of me, running her hand through my hair as we both received a wood-shaving shower.

I smiled at the memory.

I ran the sander back and forth, adjusting the grit to a smoother finish after each pass. Streaks of golden yellows and vibrant auburn shone through. I couldn't help the satisfied smile trespassing on my face.

We arranged for a real estate agent to come by on Thursday morning, which left us two days to finish the bathroom, kitchen cupboards, and most of the planting.

I thought it was optimistic while Lily thought it possible—

like everything else in life she chose to tackle. Her optimism was absolutely contagious, and it gave me the confidence to persevere.

"Here you are, my sexy carpenter." She smiled, holding two glasses of bubbly water with sliced lemon.

"Aren't you a sight for sore eyes?" She smiled, and I tried to ignore the lighthearted feeling she gave me whenever she was near. I brushed off the shavings of wood on my clothing and hair.

"Let me." She set down the glasses and walked over to me.

I watched how she dusted me off, starting from my head and down my shirt and arms. Everything about her touch soothed me. "Well, I could get used to that."

Her gaze met mine. Uncertainty brewed behind her baby blues, and the last thing I wanted to do was give her false hope. She deserved the goddamn world.

"Or not," I added quickly. *Fuck,* I sounded utterly ridiculous. *Just shut it, you ass. You're making this harder than it already is.*

"You're going back to New York. I'm not an idiot, Blake. Let's just say it how it is and enjoy what little time we have left."

Little time we have left. Hearing her say it aloud had the opposite effect. I wanted to pull away now to protect myself. But I feared even the strongest armor would leave me wounded.

As the sun set, we watched the ocean crash and roar, eroding the shore one wave at a time. Doubt washed over me like a seismic event. Sitting on a rock in Seaview, next to Lily, was perfect. Simple and perfect. The laid-back lifestyle, the people, the vibe—it was the opposite of New York.

New York was a money-making twenty-four-seven machine designed to keep you on the hamster wheel. But both worlds fit—my world with Lily and my world in New York.

Taking a handful of sand, I let it pass through my fingers. Her hand rested comfortably on my thigh as we sat in silence, staring vacantly at where the Pacific Ocean blurred into the horizon.

I turned to Lil. Every time I did, a million memories came flooding in. Tonight was no different. "Do you remember our first kiss?" I asked, noticing her cheeks and the tip of her nose turn rosy from the evening chill. I shouldered out of my jacket and placed it around her shoulders.

"Of course, Blake." She smiled, but there was an undercurrent of sadness in her tone I couldn't ignore.

She was sad things were coming to an end, just like I was. But there was no other way.

"Bet you didn't know I wanted to kiss you that entire time I was showing you how to stand up on your surfboard."

She squeaked out a laugh. "Really?"

"It's true. You were wearing a red and white polka-dot bikini with these flimsy tie things that I thought could come loose at any moment. In fact, if there weren't other people in the sea, I wanted to toss them out of their flimsy knots."

She laughed. "I bet you did."

"I think we were in the water for four hours that day. It was torture! Me being behind you, steadying the board all that time."

She rolled her eyes. "So sorry I wasn't Kelly Slater."

"The torture wasn't teaching you how to surf," I cried out. "It was having to get a rear view of your delicious ass each time you tried getting up when a wave rolled in."

She chuckled, and it reverberated through my chest. "If it makes you feel any better, I memorized the water dripping down your abs, one crevice at a time." Her eyes shone in the dusk light.

I grinned. "You did, did you?"

Her lips twisted in a smile.

I clasped my hands around her chin as her eyes leveled me with one look. "Look, over there." I turned her head toward the cave behind us. "Want to make out with me, Ms. Stone?"

"You're so juvenile." She rolled her eyes, but her mouth edged into a grin.

I yanked her up with both hands and set off for the cave. Soon, walking turned into running, and as I reached out for her hand, she took it, the wind slapping us in the face. I glanced at Lil. I thought I'd committed her to memory, but damn, she was something else. Her hair curled around her neck, her smile large and carefree.

I pulled her into the opening of the cave. "This is the spot, right here," I said, pinning her against the wall. "You were right here in your string bikini, I was in my blue and white board shorts, and we were dripping wet."

She stared at me like she had this innate ability to see straight through me. The darkness swallowed our bodies. The moonlight shone into the cave opening, lighting up the soft contours of her face. "I knew if I kissed you then, that would have been it. We would jeopardize the best friendship I've ever had, but I was willing to blow it all to hell to taste you, Lily. You were like a drug, and I needed my fix."

"As were you, Blake." She dug her hands into my back pockets and closed the gap between us.

"Fuck, I've missed you." I tilted my head down, her eyes like deep pools of water. Slowly, my lips found hers, desperately longing and kissing her with everything I had.

The kiss was slow and sensual, heating every part of my body. I cupped her cheek, savoring every bit of her as our bodies melded into one. She removed her hands from my jeans pockets and circled them around my neck. Yearning bloomed inside me, and I deepened our kiss. My heart expanded with a longing I didn't want to let go of.

She removed her lips from mine, hesitation flickering across her face. "Blake."

Drunk in her eyes, I stared, wanting more of her. "Yes."

"I think we should go." Her gaze steadied.

She snapped me out of my love-sick coma or whatever the hell that was. "Right. Yes. Big day tomorrow."

* * *

While she slept soundly, I lay awake beside her in her bed.

Realizing I'd completely forgotten the whereabouts of my phone, I fumbled out of bed and into the living room.

God, where's the goddamn lamp switch again? With tentacle arms, I felt around until I found the switch. The room filled with warm light, and between the pottery and artwork on the shelf, I located my phone.

Shit.

Robert's name flashed too many times to count. There must be a problem at work. *Fuck.* Pressure welled in my chest, and I shook my head. Everything was fine two hours ago when I checked in.

I clicked his name and exhaled loudly. It rang once before he picked up.

"Where the fuck have you been?" he snapped down the line.

"What's wrong, Robert?"

"Your fiancé, my daughter, is what's wrong. She was photographed canoodling with Chase Reynolds."

"The ex-bachelor?"

"I don't know who the fuck he is."

I laughed.

"Is that funny?" I could almost feel the steam burn coming from his ears.

"Well, she's your daughter, Rob. Surely, you know she's not faithful."

"I don't give a fuck what happens behind closed doors, but in public, my reputation is everything."

And so is mine.

Uh-huh. Of course, that's what you're worried about. Not that your daughter is an attention-seeking addict.

"I've booked the Plaza for three weeks."

"What?" *No, he didn't.*

"We need to put a leash on her. Marrying her ought to settle her down for a while."

"I don't think anything will settle Camille down, Rob. And not to mention, that would have to be the world's shortest engagement."

"Too bad."

Three weeks? The hairs on my arms stood up. Suddenly, this was becoming all too real. "She won't go for it," I argued.

"If she wants her inheritance, she will."

"What if I don't want it?"

"I'm sending the prenup over now. Marry her within the month, and you can manage the firm's three-billion-dollar portfolio."

"You're serious?"

"When have you ever seen me kid around? You've earned it anyway. You shit all over the portfolio managers here. You know that, Blake."

My mind swirled as I quickly did the math. With bonuses, that was an eight-figure salary.

Eight fucking figures.

It was everything I ever wanted. Then why did my stomach tug like a ball and chain?

"Well?" he said, growing impatient.

"You don't kid around. Ever." My voice was low.

"Good. I'll see you on Sunday. I've got my PR team drafting the announcement that will go out tomorrow."

"My flight lands at four in the morning."

"Good, come straight to the office. I'll arrange to have your team in for a six o'clock briefing."

Fuck. "Okay."

The phone went dead. And I stood, for I don't know how long, staring at the blank screen.

Eight figures and lead portfolio manager. My legs carried me toward the bedroom. Careful not to wake Lily, I slowly opened the door. I hovered in the doorframe, watching her sleep. She didn't sleep with window furnishings, rather enjoying waking up to nature, so the moonlight spread its light into the room. She murmured something. I noticed she did that when she was in a deep sleep.

The sheet patterned with flowers wrapped around her naked body. Her strawberry blonde hair curled underneath her chin, her lips crimson, and her skin invitingly creamy. *Damn.*

I was doing the right thing. What Lil and I had was fleeting. Love was a fool's game at best.

All I had to do was marry Camille. It was a marriage of convenience that worked in everyone's favor.

Then, why was I now doubting everything?

16

LILY

The grass scraped my bare ankles, wet from the early morning dew. I strolled up and down the orchard, breathing a fresh lungful of the morning air. A swarm of bees hovered near the apple blossoms, collecting their share of pollen.

The winter crop Al and I planted was now producing. At least, the new owners would reap the rewards.

I opened the wooden door to the chicken coop, and the hens flocked toward me as though they hadn't seen food for a week. I threw out some discarded scraps from the kitchen and watched as they fought to their near death. Then I scooped up the fresh eggs and placed them in my basket, grateful for everything in my life.

My days here were limited. I trudged back up past the row of kale, my shoulders caving inward. I'd miss this place so much. It was so much more than a house, it was my sanctuary. My place of discovering who I was without my parents, learning and trying a multitude of new things and living each day as though it were my last. It was where I fell in love with the boy next door.

The same boy lying in my bed and leaving me again in a few days. Neither of us had spoken about his impending flight. But last night, in the cave, I wondered if maybe there was a chance he'd stay. It was in his kiss. It felt like I was the only woman he would ever kiss again. There was no one, no time, and no space between us, just us and the cave that cocooned us. I hesitated when his kiss left me weak in the legs.

Self-preservation kicked in, and I did what I had to do and pulled away first. I made the excuse to leave as it was getting late. But the reality was so much different. I found it hard to breathe. Suffocated by the emotion of what we'd become in such a short space of time, the reality of him leaving me once again was a sucker punch to the gut.

I pulled the gate shut to the orchard, sucking in another lungful of crisp fall air. Fear replaced the serenity I'd felt moments ago. I steadied myself against the gate. *When he leaves, I don't think I'll be okay.* I wasn't angry. I couldn't be. I knew exactly what I was doing going into this, but I couldn't fight my feelings. I hated what I would feel when he was gone.

Empty.

Like when my parents were ripped from me. And just like a curse, it was happening again.

When I rounded the kitchen counter, I heard the stream of running water. Something stopped me from stripping down and sliding in next to him, but only just. Part of me wanted to savor every moment with him, but starting to distance myself was the sensible thing to do.

Too late for that.

Maybe I was just a hopeless romantic, holding onto hope like the fraying thread it was. He didn't love his fiancé, and she certainly didn't love him. It was all for show. A business arrangement where everyone got their end. *Except me.*

I cracked the eggs into a jug, whisking the pale yellows to a light and fluffy consistency. The melted butter bubbled in the frying pan as I poured in the eggs with a handful of fresh garden spinach, bell peppers, sliced pancetta, and feta cheese. Butter caramelized the edges of the omelet, the consistency of egg, changing from liquid to solid bubbles.

"Good morning, beautiful." The smell of clean laundry invaded my senses as Blake leaned down, kissing me on the cheek.

I leaned into him, wrapping my arms around his narrow waist. He breathed in my hair, then pulled away, leaving me missing him already. "You okay?" I asked.

"Yes, fine." He flashed me a smile, but it didn't reach his eyes, then he looked past me. "Something smells amazing."

Hesitant to ruffle whatever time we had left by peppering him with questions, I turned off the stove and served breakfast. "Here we have a fresh garden omelet."

He sat at the counter. Ripped jeans clung to his thick thighs, and a fitted black T-shirt had me staring at his corded tanned muscles. It was torture being this close and even harder to try and forget his tongue between my thighs.

"Thanks, Lil," he said, taking a mouthful. "Today, I was thinking of painting the outside of the house." He kept his gaze on the plate in front of him.

I blinked, unsure I heard him correctly. "But, I thought you confirmed the contractor for outside?"

"I canceled him. Best if I knock it off. We're ahead of schedule anyway, right?"

"I thought we could do the kitchen together?" *Stop sounding so desperate.*

"You don't need me for that, do you?"

Disappointment ran through me. "I guess not." He was pulling away, and there wasn't a damn thing I could do about it. I exhaled, trying to steady my trembling hand.

We ignored the elephant in the room at breakfast, and he left me alone for the entire morning. He worked outside, not checking in like he had done previously and dotting me with kisses and feels. Fine. Whatever. I managed perfectly fine on my own. Always had.

The walls weren't the only thing separating us. It seemed like we were worlds apart, even though he was just outside. Last night he kissed me like he loved me, and today, I was no one. *Again.*

Standing back, I admired my handiwork. Freshly painted white cupboards with matte black door knobs revived the old, unhinged kitchen doors. It looked like a brand-new kitchen.

My phone vibrated. I could hear it, but when I looked around, I couldn't find it. The damn thing was a nuisance. Maybe I ought to get rid of it. The thought intrigued me.

I inched closer to the piercing ring. Buried underneath a painting tray, I quickly reached for it before it stopped. "Hello?"

"Lily, is that you?" The voice sounded familiar, but I couldn't place it.

"This is Lily. Who's this?"

"It's Brennan. I'm in Seaview. I thought we could meet up while I'm in town."

"Brennan, hello." *Did I misread his email?* I didn't have a meetup scheduled on my calendar.

"Um, now?"

"I'm in town today only. Then have to head back to the city. I have a meeting at Shady Palms now, so meet me in half an hour? I'll be finished up by then."

"Shady Palms?" It was the trendiest place on High street. "Sure, that should be fine."

I'm sure Blake wouldn't even miss me.

I placed the screwdriver on the bench and walked outside to where Blake had been working.

"Kitchen's done, Blake. I've just got to head into town for a bit. I'll bring you back some lunch?"

154

"Okay, sure." He rolled the last section of gray paint. Sweat wet his black shirt, and it clung to his carved chest.

Okay, stop looking.

I turned toward the house.

Wow.

It was completely transformed from peeling paint and broken boards that held the house together just two weeks ago. "It's looking amazing," I added.

"Thanks." He didn't even look at me. Instead, he continued rolling like I wasn't even there.

My lips pressed together, and I straightened as I walked out the front gate.

Well, thank you for making it that much easier to walk out and leave you behind.

* * *

Watching as Brennan finished his meeting, I sat at the bar. It was a rather perplexing picture. Brennan's hair was perfectly in place, he was clean-shaven, and he wore an expensive suit. He was the complete opposite of his guest. Covered in tattoos and piercings, the man opposite him, with his legs wide and hunched back, didn't look like someone Brennan associated with. And I only know that because Blake told me firsthand how the prick treated him growing up. All because Blake was on a scholarship and not a true rich kid that belonged at Knights Grammar. The only reason Brennan befriended Blake was because the girls at school started to notice him.

Maybe Brennan had come around. Learned to treat everyone the same, irrespective of background and status. There was hope for him, after all.

Apparently finished, he smiled and signaled for me to come over. His smile, as I remembered, lips thin and large teeth. Black spikey hair with a sharp nose and angular jawline. He was good-looking in a preppy kind of way. Most girls would find him attractive, especially if he still carried that large-as-life persona he'd tried on me all those years ago.

I walked past the hanging potted plants with cascading ferns. Wooden tables were littered with beachgoers and tourists. Rustic milk boxes and vintage velvet chairs decorated the restaurant.

"Lily," he greeted.

"How have you been, Brennan?" I extended my hand, but he held out his arms for a hug instead. I leaned in, awkward as hell. He held onto me, squeezing me closer into his chest. Slowly, I wriggled free as politely as I could.

"Sit down. What can I get you?"

"A peppermint tea would be fine, thanks."

"Excuse me?" he yelled to no one in particular.

I shrunk into the back of my seat. *Did he just yell across a packed restaurant?*

When a server neared, he didn't even acknowledge them. "One triple espresso and a peppermint tea." His eyes were large like saucers, lapping up the attention.

Nothing's changed.

"Great, fabulous, actually. I head up the international hedge fund Hybrid Capital in Brisbane, and I just bought the Urus."

"The Urus?"

He laughed. "It's a Lamborghini, Lily."

Wanka. "Of course it is."

"How about you?"

"Between floristry and digital marketing, I'm just here enjoying the—"

"I can't tell you how nice it is to see you, Lily," he said, cutting me off.

"Thanks, you too, Brennan."

The waiter he yelled at earlier now placed our order on the table, a scowl of epic proportions tattooed on his face.

"Thank you so much," I apologized in a whisper, and he smiled slightly before turning on his heel.

"So, fancy dinner with me?"

I choked on my tea but covered it up with a cough. *Was he serious?* "Weren't you just here for a short time?"

"Plans can easily change." His eyes met mine as he took his hands and roughly rubbed the tip of his nose.

I straightened, feeling on edge at his forwardness. "Sorry, I have plans."

His hand reached for mine as it rested against the tea saucer. I froze. This wasn't right. He was hiring me for a job, and he was outright hitting on me. With the hand he was holding, I slid it away to clasp my teacup.

My skin prickled with heat, and I felt him before I saw him. *Shit.*

I watched Brennan turn toward him as I pulled my bangs over my eyes.

"Blake Carter. Where have you been? By the looks of it, in a scrap yard." Laughter rolled off Brennan's back.

Fuck's sake. If Seaview were handing out awards, Blake Carter would top the podium for sexiest tradesman on planet Earth. Paint slashed his singlet and worn jeans. His bicep muscles gleamed with sweat, and his thick hair looked messed up as though we'd just gone three rounds between the sheets. I inhaled his manly scent, and it smacked me between my thighs. My sex clenched as I drew my legs together underneath the table.

"I'm surprised they let you in here, looking like that."

Blake turned to me, completely ignoring Brennan. "What are you doing here, Lil?" His lips flattened into barely contained anger.

Instantly, guilt washed over me, yet I hadn't done anything

wrong. "That work thing I told you about. Brennan called since he was in town, so he suggested we meet up."

Blake's eyes searched mine. Etched in pain I clearly understood, he looked at me as though I had betrayed him.

"Pity she's busy for dinner too, as I'm sure we could have got a lot done." He swiped his nose as his lips turned up into a titanic-sized grin.

Oh fuck.

Blake's expression darkened. The vein in his neck throbbed. *Why was he mad?* It's not like I was doing anything with Brennan. Heck, what if I was? He was the one engaged, not me.

"You asked where I've been, Brennan?" If he was angry, he didn't show it. His voice was lethally composed. "Manhattan, but you probably knew that. What you don't know is in just under a month, I'll be the youngest man ever to be responsible for a three-billion-dollar portfolio at the little hedge fund called Jackson and Roche. You might have heard of them." He paused before adding. "And on top of that, I'll be part of the Jackson family, marrying Camille Jackson."

The teacup nearly dropped out of my hands. *Under a month? Since when? And was it just me that thought maybe he'd call the wedding off?* Anger and confusion swept through my veins like a tidal wave.

"Well, good on you…" Brennan continued to talk, but it could have been in Swahili for all I cared.

A painful lump rose in my throat as reality sunk in like a bitch. Blake, *my Blake*, was to be married in under a month. *Fuuuck!* I wanted to scream. It's all fake. She doesn't love you like I do. She cheats, but I knew it wasn't even about her. It never was. He'd been gifted the deal of the century in his eyes, and all he had to do was marry Camille.

"I'll be sure to send you an invite. It's at the Plaza."

"Can't wait." Brennan deadpanned.

Blake turned to me. His dark eyes softened when he took me in. I tried to hide the tornado inside me, but my own emotions were too raw, and I was a terrible actress. I wanted to flee. But I couldn't. Words had lost their meaning, tea its taste. *No, I'm not going to cry. Fuck's sake, I'm not.*

"Lily, I have to get some more paint. Will you come with me?" There was a pleading in his voice I had to ignore.

"No," I snapped. "I'm not done here with Brennan."

I didn't look at him. I couldn't. I just wanted him to leave.

"Lil," he said in a low voice.

I ignored Blake, giving Brennan my full focus. "So, Brennan, tell me about this project."

S he was making a ton of noise in the cottage, enough to piss off the neighbors. If she hadn't imparted the Lily charm she exuded everywhere she went, they'd be calling the cops with a noise complaint.

Maybe she'd realized meeting up with Brennan wasn't a good idea, and she was making me dinner as an apology. I knew how much she loved to cook.

Doubtful, dickhead.

I'd gone into town to get another can of paint. Sure, I could have called Lily to pick one up, but part of me wanted to bump into her, surprise her and take her out to lunch for being a bit of a dick this morning. As I strolled past the huge glass windows of the Shady Palms Café, I stopped. *Fuck. I wish I hadn't.* I could pick out her strawberry blonde bob and infectious laugh from a crowded mall. Then there was Brennan. After spending every day at school with him, his face was fucking unmistakable.

Sure, we became friends if you wanted to call it that. In the younger years, he'd thrown shade on me like I was a piece of gum under his shiny Nikes. So many times, he'd made fun of my second-hand school bag or my used school shoes that Dad had picked up from the thrift shop. My textbooks curled up at the edges and were handed down from others he'd mocked. It wasn't until I hit middle school that things started to change. I'd developed into my own skin and popped muscles, strong from all the carpentry work Dad and I did. Girls noticed me. The girls who clung to Brennan started paying me attention. Then, slowly his ridicule became less like ridicule and more like friendly banter.

One day, he invited me to sit with him and his crew, and I said yes. Of course, I wanted to be part of the popular kids' club, part of the elite at Grammar. Fitting into their club was all I'd ever wanted. At first, I'd become closer with his best friends, Fabian and Rocky. But over time, Brennan and I hung out, and I'd put aside the bullshit he threw at me in my younger years. The four of us were invincible—Brennan, Fabe, Rocky, and me. The hottest girls in school wanted to be around us. Teachers didn't dare look twice at us for fear of the weight of their rich parents. And if I was in that crew, I too was protected.

But even though I had it all, even the hottest girl on her knees in my final year, I wanted Lily. It took my party to realize it. It took watching a dickhead like Brennan try and take advantage of a tipsy Lily. He moved in, like a panther to prey, to try and kiss her. Even when she'd said no, he persisted. That's when I snapped.

Years later, he was the same arrogant fuck who had his hand on hers again. And she still looked as uncomfortable as she did at that party in my backyard. Standing by and watching wasn't in my DNA. I wanted to launch at the cunt and plow into him, breaking his pointed nose again like the night he kissed her against her will. But I didn't. It wouldn't be a fair fight, seeing as the asshole was high as a fucking kite. In my line of work, I could tell a coke-head a mile away.

I exhaled and closed my laptop, admiring the new and improved kitchen Lily had finished this morning. But that didn't last long. I couldn't erase the image of Brennan's hand on hers, and my mind swirled as my breath hitched in my rib cage. Irritation coursed through my veins, and I went from calm to explosive in a nanosecond.

When I flung open the fly-screen door, it boomeranged straight back, and I shouldered it out of the way. I didn't give a fuck. I marched along the pathway toward the cottage, fire in each stride. Brennan's slimy hand was on hers. *Had she told him the arrangement of Dad's will?*

She wouldn't. *Fuck, man. Get a grip, man.*

I marched into the cottage. Sitting opposite her laptop, Lil lowered it when our eyes connected. "What the hell was that, Blake?" She steepled her hands across the counter, eyes narrowing to the size of peanuts. *Why was she mad at me?* "Why didn't you tell me your wedding was within the month?"

Dammit. The look on her face the moment I'd let that slip was like a sucker punch to the gut. I was so consumed with what was going on with her and Brennan, I'd completely forgotten I had let the wedding date slip. Either that, or I just pushed it away, trying to forget about my impending doom.

"I just found out last night," I murmured.

"How can you just find out something like that? That's something you plan. As a little girl, it's something you dream about. It's not something that you just decide overnight."

"It's complicated, Lil. You wouldn't understand."

"Try me." She folded her arms, her gaze relentless.

"Well, obviously, you know I'm engaged to Camille."

"Yes, Einstein."

Okay, sure, I deserved that.

"Her Dad rang me, she's up to no good again, and he wants me to put a lid on it before it wrecks his reputation and his entire empire." Fuck, just saying it out loud sounded absurd. Yet, I straightened my back.

"So you marry her, and what? Keep her in a gilded cage?"

"Something like that."

"Do you even love her?"

Hell no. "I'm not sure that's even relevant."

She lowered her hands, throwing them down by her side. "Do you hear yourself, Blake Carter? Of course, it's relevant." A throaty grunt left her mouth, and my muscles tensed like steel.

"Maybe in your world, but in mine, it's not all princes and princesses getting their happy ever after."

"My world?" She bit back. "Don't you mean ninety-nine percent of the population who actually want love or to be loved?"

Fuck's sake, why couldn't she see this from my point of view?

I couldn't deal with this now. I was the one with the questions, not her. "How about you and Brennan? That looked cozy. What did I interrupt?"

She laughed, and a vein in my neck ticked. "You're not serious?"

"Deadly." I was fucking fuming.

"You did interrupt something, but not what you think. We were in a business meeting."

"You're kidding, right?" Smoke billowed from my ears. "He had his hand on yours?"

She stared at me although she wanted to say something but didn't. "You have no damn right to say anything about who I talk to, Blake." Her lips rolled into a thin line, and I knew she was just as angry with me.

"Fair point. But don't lie to me, Lily. Of all the people in my life, *you* can't lie to me."

Confusion swept over her features. *Had she no clue what I was talking about?* "Did you tell him he gets the house if I leave before the two weeks is up?"

"What? she yelled. "No! Are you serious right now?"

Why did that thought even cross my mind? My head had been playing tricks on me since I got back to Seaview. My hand lifted to my forehead. "I don't know anymore."

"Do you really think I'd do that to you, Blake?" Her eyes glossed over, and I immediately regretted asking her. I wanted to hold her close, nuzzle in the crook of her neck, and make love to her just to forget about the entire day.

"No, I don't. I'm sorry." I checked my watch. "The real estate agent is due any minute. Can you come up to the house with me, please?" I glanced at her sincerely but utterly confused at my jealous outburst.

"Fine." She stood and brushed past me.

"Fine?"

"That's all I have to give you right now, Blake." She walked a step ahead of me, and I trailed behind. I didn't want my last days here like this. I wanted them wrapped up in her arms where I ought to be. But that didn't remotely look like it was going to happen. And it was probably for the best anyway. It would make leaving easier.

Fuck, who was I kidding?

* * *

"Lily, Blake, what you've done with this place in such a short period is astonishing. The place is light, bright, and so modern. The kitchen facelift, the boards outside, it's restored to its former glory." Roger, our realtor from Property Central, had left his jaw on the floor as he walked around the house for the second time.

"You probably don't know this, but I was here a few months ago. I was on the same street appraising another property, and Alistair was out the front and invited me in for a coffee and a chat."

"I did, actually. That's why you're here and not Carl from Seaview Property." Lily glanced at me sideways. It was the first time she'd acknowledged me in what seemed like forever, and Roger flipped me a nervous smile.

Yes, I may have been halfway across the world and manic busy, but I always made time for my old man and our weekly phone calls.

"Take a seat, please." I sat down on the restored Parker couch and invited him to sit on the chair opposite.

"Right, and I appreciate that, Blake."

"Relax, Roger. You've got the listing."

He cleared his throat, a showy smile lifting on his face. "Wonderful, thank you." He stared between us. "Can I state the bleeding obvious here?"

My heart rate spiked as I found myself gripping the couch cushion. I lowered my gaze to Lily, who'd positioned herself on the seat the furthest away from me, a distantly cool expression rolling over her face.

What was I afraid of, the truth?

"You could be a renovation team on one of those television shows."

The relief came out in laughter. "Thanks, but I think we'll just go back to our respective jobs now."

He shrugged, casting his eyes around the restored house. "Shame. You guys really have something here. Sure the block size is huge, and the proximity to the beach is fantastic, but I've seen a few houses in my time, and this renovation is the best yet. At least think about teaming up to do more?"

My eyes met Lil's, who gave nothing away.

"Sure." I smiled, placating him.

"So, I understand you and Lily are both the rightful owners?"

"Yes, we are."

"I see. Well, I see no problems in selling this house. It would be a family's dream to live here."

"Fine," I agreed. "I just want it sold."

"Of course. I can arrange for the floor plan and pictures to be taken next week," Roger said.

"If it's as good as Roger says it is, Blake, you may actually get a good price, in respect for Al," Lily said.

"We will do our best to get the best price possible. But it's good to know you're not hung up on it," Roger said.

"Hung up?" She let out a loud exhalation. "You might want to give it away, Blake, but Al would be livid if he heard you speak that way."

So now she wants to talk.

"Maybe you're right. But I don't need the money," I replied.

"And I do?" She pushed away her tea saucer, and it scraped across the coffee table.

Roger glanced between Lily and me. "I'll just give you two a moment."

Fucking great. He walked out the back door, and we both waited to speak until it shut behind him.

"Well, let's be honest, you could do with the money. You were living in the cottage out back."

Okay, that came off worse than I expected.

Her blue eyes widened. "How dare you. I'm not saying that because I want the money. I couldn't give a rat's ass about it. I'd gladly give it all back if it's what you wanted. This is for your dad and the pride he took living here and caring for his yard."

Dammit. I rubbed my forehead. "Sorry, I know. I don't know what I'm saying anymore. I just have a lot on my plate at the moment. I just want the house to be sold. Then it's one less thing to worry about."

"So you can go back to your perfect life?" she teased, leaning back in her chair, her eyes leveling me with her accusation.

The hairs stuck up on the back of my neck. "Lily, please." My fingers threaded my hair, tugging at the ends. I hated how she was drilling me into a corner, but at the same time, I had evaded the truth long enough.

"Anyway, let's not leave the realtor waiting any longer." She gave a slight headshake.

"Okay." I shrugged. "Roger?"

He opened the door and wandered in. You could cut the tension with a knife.

I stood, signaling the meeting was over. "Thanks for coming, Roger."

"Of course. One last question. Will you be living in the cottage when the viewings are on, Lily?"

A frown etched across her forehead. "Well, if you start immediately, I guess I—"

"Tell me you have somewhere to go, Lil?" I asked, exasperated. *Had she not even considered moving out till now?*

"Yes, I'm sure I'll find something." Her eyes darted from side to side.

"You don't actually have to move during the showings, you know," Roger said.

She looked at me, and I couldn't hide the shock on my face if I tried. "That's okay. I think it will be better presented if I'm not here."

"What without your Pilates machine, pottery, and art collection?" A grin peeled on my face as she narrowed her eyes. *Fuck, really?* It was a joke.

"Just stay, Lil," I pleaded.

"No, it's fine," she snapped.

I hovered in the doorframe as Roger glanced between us.

"It's okay. I'll sort it out," she insisted.

"We will sign the paperwork and get it back to you today."

"Excellent. I'll be sure to make your dad proud," he said, and I believed him.

He grabbed his portfolio and notes he'd made as Lily showed him out. I hung back, watching her. Everything about her I loved and hated at the same time.

How was that fucking possible?

"Right, well, that's done." She stood awkwardly in the hall-way, hands hanging loose by her sides.

"Listen, Lil. I didn't mean that stuff about your pottery."

"Do you think it's all junk?" She looked hurt, and I wanted to take back everything I'd said.

"No, of course not. You're very talented."

"Well, you obviously have an opinion about it." She folded her arms across her waist. It inched up her T-shirt, revealing her flat stomach, and once again, my eyes were drawn to her. "Go on."

My eyes flickered up to hers. "It doesn't matter, Lily. None of it matters."

She exhaled and shook her head. "I think it's been a busy two weeks. I'm going to do some more planting in the yard. Join me if you want. Or not." A shrug rolled over her shoul-ders. "I don't care at this point." She walked out toward the backyard, not looking behind her.

I walked over to the kitchen stool and watched her outside, my chest constricting with each breath. The sun was setting, and all I could think about was leaving her tomorrow. Leaving her and returning home—to Manhattan.

Confusion leveled me helpless, so I did what I did best and went to work. I opened my laptop and scoured my emails. My schedule was full. My executive assistant had filled my first week back with meeting after meeting. *Gah.* Sure, I was expected to hit the ground running from my lengthy absence, but seeing not even an inch of breathing room turned my insides out.

No more morning surfs or walks through the orchard soaking up the Vitamin D. Definitely no more carpentry work and the earthy smell of wood turning in the lathe. I pounded the keyboard, taking out my frustration while responding to emails.

Then I clicked on the final email, from her, of all people.

From: Camille Jackson

Dear hubby-to-be,

I heard the news. Daddy wants us wed in under four weeks. How convenient for him. I'll arrange it, just turn up.

I'm going to live at my penthouse during the week, and on weekends, we can stay in your apartment so we can appear as a couple for the press.

Welcome to the family.

Camille.

What the fuck?

I felt numb. But this was the deal I'd gotten into, and now, I was getting sucked underneath the water without a life raft.

Pushing away my computer, I thrust out my stool. Standing at the back door, I watched her, bent over, the sun at her back, setting in the distance. She hummed a tune, and it sounded like home.

Lily went about her work with a contagious freedom, and I was jealous. I wanted that feeling, the feeling I had when I was around her, and tingles shot up my arms and legs.

She was everything I wanted but everything I couldn't have. And losing her was no longer a mere probability but a damn certainty.

I couldn't bear to think about tomorrow's flight. It was too damn painful. It didn't make any sense, none of it. She put the color in my rainbow, and if fleeting, I'll take it. I needed her *now*.

I slung open the door and flew toward her. She turned just as my hand circled her waist, spinning her around into my chest. She looked up at me in surprise, and I bent down, crashing my lips to hers. It only took a moment for her to respond. She opened for me, taking her hands to the nape of my neck and kissing me back. Our tongues intertwined as my breath grew ragged and more desperate. Too soon, she pulled back and took me in.

"Hey," I said, my voice thick.

Lily studied me, and I was sure she saw straight through me. She knew me so well. And she knew this was goodbye. I watched as she swallowed down the lump in her throat. "Hey, yourself."

I kissed her again, this time deeper, her lips whiskey to my heartache. She kissed me back with a fury that matched mine. I lifted her, and she crisscrossed her legs around my waist, inter-twining her fingers around my neck

"Blake Carter, I might not like you right now, but that doesn't mean I don't need you." She rubbed up and onto my groin as her teeth pinched her lower lip.

Oh, holy hell. How could I say goodbye?

* * *

Laying her down on the bed, I wriggled down her shorts and ripped off her T-shirt. She lay in a sports bra and thong—still far too clothed for my liking. Quickly, I slid down the zipper on the front of her sports bra, and her full delicious breasts tumbled free. Like a savage, I took her nipple in my mouth, sucking it hard and dragging my teeth across it. *Slow down, Blake, savor her. Savor everything about her.*

I pulled back, wanting this moment to be perfect. She stared at me with half-hooded eyes and something else. "What is it, Blake?" she breathed out

I stared into her blue eyes, desperate to tell her how she made me feel. But there was no point. Tomorrow I'd be gone, and she deserved so much more. "Nothing," I whispered, nudging her nose with my own.

Running a hand down her cheek, I kissed her again and trailed my fingers down between her thighs. I needed more of her. Skimming the fabric of her thong, I slipped one finger underneath the material and dipped it inside her pussy. A groan escaped my throat. "Lil, your so wet."

I slowed it down, entering her with one, then two thick fingers. She moaned, leaning into my touch, and I stole her moans with a wet hot kiss. Dragging her wetness up to her ball of nerves, I slowly massaged her clit, and she bucked under my touch. Fuck, I needed all of her.

"Please," she begged, her breaths sharp and ragged. "I need you now."

Her words made my heart roar inside my chest. Quickly, I legged out of my jeans while she tugged at my briefs, sliding them over my ass and down my legs. She watched as my dick, hard for her, sprung free and rested against my stomach. I clawed back onto the bed, resting my elbows beside her head, then I lowered into her. Our eyes connected as I took large, deep, savoring breaths. "Fuck, Lil," I hissed out on a breath.

She kissed my neck, her hands around my back, in my hair, trailing down my spine. Her touch made me forget everything.

I peppered her with kisses up her neck and back to her mouth. My heart hammered louder in my rib cage as emotion shook all my senses. Everything in my body screamed alive, and I stopped, staring down at her. "Lily, I…"

A rush of panic crossed her face. "Blake, don't stop." She gasped, and immediately I ground my hips back into hers, stretching her completely.

We both knew it was for the best. I closed out my feelings. Whatever realization I had was fleeting and didn't matter.

Fast, deep thrusts followed until we were both teetering on the edge, savoring each other for the last time. She squeezed my bicep with her nails and balled the sheet in the other, then her eyes collided with mine as we both unraveled together. I committed this moment to memory and lowered my forehead to hers.

Committing this moment and the last two weeks we shared to memory.

I rolled onto my back, trying to claw at any scrap of oxygen I could.

"Oh, Blake." She turned to me, but I couldn't say anything. My breath was shot. It was thick and heavy like the room had just been sucked of all its oxygen. Her cheeks glowed, and fuck, she was so gorgeous it hurt. "That was a surprise. One minute I was gardening, the next, I'm tangled beneath you." I caressed her cheek with the pads of my fingers, and she momentarily closed her eyes. "That's what I love about you, Blake."

A sudden and overwhelming panic filled my bloodstream. She flicked open her eyes, and I stared at her with wide eyes. My chest tightened, and alarm bells sounded in my head as I fixed my stare on the ceiling. Our moment of absolute and utter euphoria erased the second she'd mentioned that fucking four-letter word.

I shot up quicker than I ought to and slipped on my briefs, then jeans. Her hand landed on my arm. "Hey, you okay?" Her voice trembled.

"Of course." I put my hand on hers and unhooked it from my arm. "I've just got a ton of emails to get back to."

Where was my fucking shirt?

18

LILY

The moment I slipped out the L-word was the instant he'd completely detached.

Why did I have to say it? But dammit, I couldn't hide it anymore. I was beyond apologizing for my actions. How could I apologize for the way I truly felt? I never had. *Why start now?* I loved Blake Carter—always had.

But he couldn't run quicker away from me after we'd just made love because what we did was exactly that. There was a moment when I thought he'd say he loved me. But maybe I was wrong. Because as soon as I said it, he couldn't get out of my house fast enough.

He'd legged into his pants and slipped on his T-shirt, then said he had emails and disappeared in the house under the guise of work calls.

Fuck me. Was his life over there so much better than here? Was it that perfect, or was I imperfect?

I stayed awake all night, tossing and twisting the sheets around my body, trying to get comfortable until I realized no matter how much I tossed and turned, I wouldn't get there. Fed up, I got up and browsed the local house rentals for a new place to live, trying to get my mind off the man who had stolen my heart not once but twice and didn't seem to care.

It only took a few clicks. I'd found a neat little studio in my price range on the outskirts of town. *Small but compact.* That's what the description read. It would never be the cottage over-looking the orchard. Nothing could replace that, but in time, I'd make it my home. I'd adapt. *I always did.*

At three in the morning, I sent off an online application without even seeing the place. It wasn't like I had the luxury of time or budget. We'd both signed off on the realtor's contract, and Roger had emailed us dates for photographers and decora-tors with the view to hold the first open house next week.

Blake would be in New York, and I'd be moved out. Both house and cottage would be empty, and that would be it. No more Blake. No best friend. He'd be fine, and I'd be a damn wreck.

* * *

Blake was leaving today, and he had avoided me most of the day. Perhaps making blinding love last night was enough. It was intense and heartbreaking, his own wordless goodbye.

When would he even come to say goodbye? I busied myself in the orchard. Pulling out the last of the weeds as they somehow shot through the thick bed of mulch. I walked the length of the market rows, noticing the seedheads sprouting above the soil line. The last few hours hadn't changed my mood, and as I finished preparing the garden for the new owners, my eyes began to gloss over. I'd resigned myself to the fact he wasn't coming out.

I exhaled as I stared at the newly finished house. But the sadness was quickly replaced with annoyance and anger. It was after two now, and he'd be leaving soon to catch his evening flight. He was ignoring me. But I wasn't another notch on his belt, for fuck's sake. If this was the last time I was to see him, he was going to leave on my terms.

My veins pumped with heated blood as my tired legs burst into a new lease on life. I stormed out the gate and toward the house, then swung open the back door to find him sitting at the kitchen counter, laptop open with his suitcase beside him, ready to go. His passport and wallet were neatly stacked beside his phone. He was set. I had no doubt that from the position he sat in, he saw me outside in the orchard. The hope I'd held onto that he was holed up in his bedroom vanished. The cold hard truth was that he just didn't give a fuck about me.

My irritation turned into something unexplainable.

"You all right?" He glanced up at me.

Each second ticked away, and his indifference clawed me until I had no more layers left. I was seething red, raw. I felt exposed, like a one-night stand with zero attachment.

"No, Blake. I'm not," I snapped, steadying myself against the kitchen counter. He lowered his laptop lid, waiting for me to continue. "I thought you would have spent today with me." I straightened against the sharp edge of the counter, my muscles tensing like balls of lead.

He stared at me vacantly. "Sorry, I had a ton of emails to get back to, a conference call, then Camille called."

I shook my head, unable to understand what I was hearing.

He tilted his head to the side. "Come on, Lily. You knew what this was."

The fact that he seemed over this was just mind-blowing. My heart thudded in my ears as my skin tingled with heat. "You're right. I knew exactly what this was. And I was dumb enough to fall for it again. I thought you changed, Blake, but was I wrong."

He pointed the pad of his finger into his strong chest. "I *might* have changed? I think out of both of us, I am the one who has changed. You're still flapping about like you have zero responsibility, living day by day. One week it's pottery, the next it's floristry, then—"

"And what's wrong with that?" I yelled, throwing my hands to the sky.

"Nothing if you're doing it for the right reasons, but I remember a carefree girl who actually wanted to do something with her life. Not bounce around from one thing to the next without a commitment and living paycheck to paycheck."

"I'm not bouncing around!" I crossed my hands across my chest.

He stared at me point blank, not saying a word.

"Okay, maybe I am a little, so what? I don't want to be tied down to one thing. I like having the freedom to pick and choose what I do. Anyway, at least I'm not the one running away."

He shook his head. "I'm not running away, Lil. I'm going home."

"To New York."

"Yes, it is my home now."

"Only because you've avoided Seaview. You've avoided me like you did the night you took my virginity. You ran then too."

He winced at the memory as a pained expression flashed on his face. "You don't think I regretted leaving you in the middle of the night?

"No. I don't know."

"I did that because if I'd stayed, I would have never left you, Lily."

His words rendered me speechless. I fucking knew we had something all along, and he threw it away.

He closed his eyes, then opened them. "I have to marry Camille."

I snapped out of my head. "You don't have to do a damn thing. You're marrying Camille to cement your future."

I watched his jaw tick. "And what's wrong with that then?" He stood and started pacing the room.

"Are you hearing yourself, Blake? You should get married because you love someone. Don't let your mom leaving ruin your outlook on love. Don't let your fear of being no one dictate your future. Because the Blake I knew was never scared of anything."

"I'm not scared, Lily." He let out a long exhale. "It's different over there. This happens all the time. If I don't do this, I'll lose everything I've worked so hard for in the last six years."

"No, who you are is the person who surfs, the person who loves the feel of wood in his hands. The person who does not devote his life to the office and enjoys time to himself."

"That's the dream, but it's not the reality. So is love."

"How would you know? Have you even opened yourself up to the possibility of love?"

He raked his hand through his hair and slumped on the barstool, and suddenly, I pitied him. He was a coward.

"Camille isn't your answer, Blake," I continued.

He kept his gaze on the ground. "I agree with you there."

A renewed sense of anger filled my veins. I just wanted to shake him and make him realize what he was diving into. "Well then, why?" I snapped.

"Because I've left this place for a reason. I've wanted to get out of Seaview, the small town with small dreams. I am bigger than that. I needed to prove to myself what I could be. I grew up with rich pricks all around me, and I was always the poor kid. I'll never ever go back to that, Lily."

"Is it as black and white as that? You've proven to yourself that you can make it. How much is enough?"

"It will never be enough. And in Seaview, there's nothing here for me." His eyes darted to mine, and he quickly opened his mouth to say something else, but nothing came out.

I turned away and swallowed down the thickness in my throat. His words smacked me in the face like the other woman I was. I steadied my trembling hand and exhaled. When I looked at him, his expression was pained and full of regret.

"You may think that, Blake, but I need to tell you, you are so wrong. I'm here. I always have been. And I love you. I have loved you since the moment we first made love all those years ago, and I still love you today."

"Lil, please," he pleaded, his lips pressing slightly together.

"I know you feel the same. It's in every touch, every smile that reaches your eyes. You need to know that you have a chance at something real with me. Don't make the same mistake twice. You know what is waiting for you on the other side of the world. And you know what you have here."

"Lily, I—"

"You don't need to say anything. Just know the moment you step out of here is the moment I will forget about you forever. I won't hold a grudge, I'll move on, and I'll adapt. And in time, I *will* find love again."

I stared at him, anguish plagued his beautiful features, but he made no attempt to move toward me.

"Lily, please don't make this any harder than it already is."

In an instant, my fragile heart shattered into thousands of tiny pieces, flooding my body with inexplicable sadness. I exhaled, and the backs of my eyes pricked with tears. "You've just given me my answer."

He pulled out his chair, and it dragged along the wooden flooring. "Wait, Lily, please understand."

I felt the touch of his hand across my wrist, but I pulled away from his grasp. "Oh, I understand perfectly." I glanced over my shoulder as a tear rolled down my cheek. "You're a coward. A fucking coward!" I cried out. His mouth fell open. "Goodbye, Blake." I turned and walked out the door, determined not to ever look back. Sobs lined my throat, and it was only when I closed the door to my cottage that I let them spill out into ugly cries.

I don't know how long had passed when my phone danced across the coffee table and lit up with an unknown number.

Clearing my throat, I wiped away the salty tears I tasted at the corners of my mouth and answered, "Hello?" My voice trembled.

"Lily Stone?"

"Yes," I said, clearing my throat again and trying to sound more like myself.

"This is Jacob. I'm managing the rental over on Clyde Avenue and wanted to call and let you know your application for the studio has been accepted."

I exhaled. "Thanks, Jacob. That's the best news I've had all day. I'm just in the middle of something. Can I call you a bit later about the details?"

"Yes, not a problem."

"Thanks." I clicked off the phone and threw it across the couch.

My eyes spilled with fresh tears I had just blotted away. I curled my chest into my knees, holding myself. It was amazing news, but my heart was broken. Wet and warm tears dripped down my legs, and I let them flow, not bothering to wipe them away.

Moving out was the final piece of the puzzle in letting him go. All the memories would simply be memories with nothing tangible to tie them to. I held my knees and buried my face, letting the emotion come, and it shook me to the bone.

It wasn't just the end of Blake and me, it was the end of this time in my life. Heartache stung like a bitch, but I clung to it, not willing to let him go yet.

19

BLAKE

Trained on me were twenty pairs of eyes. But I couldn't think, let alone try to dissect which of the four lithium companies we were looking at was the best investment. I sat in the boardroom, leading my team of analysts absentmindedly. I'd already sucked back my third espresso after disembarking from the flight and arriving at our Midtown offices.

Flying over Central Park, the Hudson River, and the Brooklyn Bridge didn't have the same thrill as it normally did.

Twenty-four hours ago, I was in Seaview. During the two weeks I'd spent there, I found an unimaginable level of relaxation. Work didn't hold the same gravity as the weight it held now.

Because that's not all I found in Seaview.

"You awake there, boss?"

I blinked, snapping back into the reality in front of me. "I'm fucking fine, don't ask me that again." The arrogant, high-collar-wearing, four-eyed prick had tried to one-up me for months now. Any opportunity, he clung to it like a bulldog, but I'd been the pillar of perfection in my role. And every time he would try to one-up me, it fell on his deadpan face like the fuckhead he was. If he weren't the cousin of one of the partners, he would have been out the door months ago.

"Right, let's move on to agenda item fourteen."

I had been in the boardroom since seven this morning, time ticked away, and before I knew it, it was now four o'clock. I was well and truly done.

My phone buzzed as the last of my team filtered out of the boardroom.

Robert's name flashed on the screen, and I slunk into my chair.

"Robert."

"Come up," he insisted, and the line went dead.

"On my way," I muttered, exiting the boardroom.

I stood waiting for the elevator doors to spring open. Desks were full of analysts and traders studying their monitors or on their phones. Ticker tape flashed across enormous wall screens with the day's roundup. The expansive room was divided into teams because we were a highly competitive bunch, not to mention Robert got off on competition.

Most of them were more interested in getting fucked by the latest model than worrying about lining their back pockets. They came from money. I didn't, and I hustled like my life depended on it. Nothing was ever enough. It was the lifeblood that flowed through my veins. Quitting was never an option. I was so driven I could have been the poster boy for a Tony Robbins seminar. But as I stepped inside the elevator and watched the doors slide shut, I wondered if, on my deathbed, I'd have any regrets.

Lily had laid it all out. She bared her soul and confessed that she loved me. But the only thing I had heard was my father's tears, distraught over my mother leaving him. That's how fucked up I was over love.

The elevator doors opened, and I stepped into the foyer

where grown men licked the blow off the tits of escorts weeks ago. Only this time, it was well lit, immaculately cleaned with no shred of debauchery.

Carl Soder, my boss, walked toward me. Well, that explains his absence from the meeting.

He flipped me the bird on his way out. "Piss off, Blake."

"What the fuck, Carl?"

Robert walked around his mahogany desk and held the door open. "Don't worry about him. He's gone."

"What?" *Had I heard him correctly?*

"Mr. Jackson, you have Aaron Mellings calling on line two," Robert's PA said.

"About time," he grumbled out. "Come in and take a seat, son."

Fucking don't call me that. I only have one dad, and you are nothing like him.

He spun on his chair and picked up the phone. "Aaron. Tell me." As each second ticked by and Robert listened to the guy on the line, his calm face changed to a deathly glare. "I don't give a fuck, Aaron." He spoke with a measured yet simmered rage. He held the receiver close. "If you don't get this done, you know what is waiting at the other end." He clicked off the phone, his face glowing with rage.

Whoever Aaron was, he was probably scared as fuck. There was no mistaking Robert's caustic undertone. It had always been there, but more so in the last six months.

"Everything all right with that phone call?"

"No, but it will be." There was a wickedness to his smile that creeped me out.

Maybe because I'd heard rumors about his links with the Manhattan mob, until now, I'd never thought it could be true. We all thought it was ridiculous rumors spread by the other firms, but now I wasn't so sure.

"Right. Sorry about your father and all that. You did what you had to over there?"

Thoughts of Lily flashed back—the feel of her skin, the way her leg hooked over my hips, and she melted into me. "Almost."

He raised an eyebrow.

I shook away the thought. "It's all done, just selling the house with the realtor, then it's final."

"Seaview, right? I don't know how anyone could ever live in the middle of nowhere. Fuck, I'd rip my balls off."

I laughed. "Yeah."

The truth was, with the new infrastructure, Seaview had become more connected than ever before. The town I'd run away from all those years ago wasn't nearly as bad as I remembered. Actually, I hadn't realized how much I missed the beach and being out in nature. And more so, being around fewer people.

"I fired Carl," he said, staring at his screen.

"How come?" I knew why. The cat was lazy as fuck.

"Lazy cunt, you were doing his job."

I leaned back in the chair. "Well, that's true."

"You read the prenup?"

"I scanned it."

His eyes came to mine. "Since when do you ever scan anything?"

Since reacquainting with a short, blonde, blue-eyed girl.

I had the opportunity so many times on the plane, but I didn't look at it, refusing to acknowledge what was happening in less than a month's time. I wanted to cling to the memory of Lily for as long as possible.

"Well, I suggest you hurry up. Did you see that if you get her pregnant, you get a ten-million-dollar bonus?"

"Yes."

"Jesus, don't seem so excited. Are you listening to yourself, or did the small town suck your dick dry?"

"No, you're right. I'm just tired, that's all."

He narrowed his eyes as deep crevices lined his face. "So sign it, get it done. We need to put the firm in a better light by getting Camille out of fucktown and into motherhood."

"You don't want to push this out? Maybe slow down a bit. Maybe she doesn't want this."

He stood. "I don't give a damn what she wants. She's been a spoiled bitch all her life, just like her mother. Now she's swanning around with her fresh tits, fucking whatever moves and snorting blow like its water."

My hands palmed skyward. "Exactly! Maybe she's not ready to settle down."

He narrowed his eyes. "Are you telling me you don't want to cement your position here in the firm and marry my daughter?"

My heart beat faster, and my brow burst into a sweat. Now was the time to get out of this. Now was the time to put my hand up like the good little boy in class and excuse myself from the fuck show that was about to grab me by the balls for the rest of my life.

"Let me remind you, your earnings here are unparalleled. We've paid you seven million in just the last year. You couldn't get that anywhere else."

I sucked in a level breath. "And I appreciate that, Robert. I'm here, aren't I?"

"Good. Now get the fuck out of here and go home."

Home.

"Oh, and check your damn phone. Camille has been trying to call you all day."

And that's why I haven't picked up. "Everything okay?"

"I don't fucking know. Do I look like your assistant?"

I let out a laugh. "No, you definitely don't." If looks could kill, I'd be dead already. I rolled my lips in, trying not to laugh. "Right, see you tomorrow." Walking to the door, I tripped over the carpet.

"What the fuck is wrong with you?"

"All good!" I joked.

Passing his secretary, I gave her a nod, smiled, and walked toward the elevator. I realized there was nothing at all funny about this situation.

The elevator door shut behind me. The caffeine tremors had worn off, and the adrenaline had waned. Now, in its place, was jetlag and sheer exhaustion.

I didn't want to check any messages from Camille, and I hoped like hell she'd kept to her word and was staying at her penthouse.

After gathering my things, I stepped into the waiting car downstairs.

* * *

My elevator doors pinged open, and I walked out into the noise. *What the?*

It was coming from my kitchen area. I walked into the lobby and past the round tables with fresh-cut flowers in a vase.

"Darling!" Camille burst forward with her arms wide. A bunch of unknown faces turned toward me. She flung her arms around me in some random show of affection that I couldn't help but laugh out loud.

"Camille, what's going on? Who are all these people in my apartment?" They all turned to me like I was the main attraction.

"Well, blow me. I didn't know he was this cute!" Laughter erupted from the group as a balding middle-aged man slowly violated me with his eyes.

"Excuse me?"

"This is Federico and Claire from Manhattan Buds. They did the flowers for Brad and Angelina. And over here are Paul and Dario from the Canape Table."

"Would you like a sample, Blake?"

A redhead with black-framed glasses thrust something fishy in my direction, and the smell turned the contents of my stomach into my throat. "No, I don't."

She tilted her head toward Camille, and I let out an exasperated sigh.

I dropped my bag and suitcase, and they thudded on the tiled floor. "I'm going to grab a scotch." I slid away from the crowd. The last thing I wanted was strange people in my apartment when I was jetlagged as fuck and not invested in this wedding one bit.

"His dad just died, so he's a tad precious."

What the actual fuck?

I stopped walking toward the bar. Camille laughed, tossing her fresh blow-wave back behind her shoulders, completely void of any emotion.

That was it. With steely determination and raging blood pressure, I marched toward my soon-to-be-wife. Conversations stopped as their eyes came to mine. Camille caught sight of me.

"What is it, Blake?" She sneered through shiny veneers.

"Show some fucking respect, Camille."

Her jaw went slack, and she looked at me wide-eyed. At least, I think she was. Her forehead didn't move an inch.

"Oh, dear. Is he normally like this?" one of the men whisper-yelled so that I could hear.

Irritation leveled me. "Right, that's it. Everyone, out."

"Blake, what is wrong with you?" she yelled.

"I'm tired. I've come off a long-haul flight and been at work all day."

She turned to face the others, her face flush with anger. They stared at me like I was wielding a trident and the goddamn devil himself. I didn't give two flying fucks and walked away.

"Perhaps, we'll do this when he's not in this mood."

Fucking hell.

Scurrying feet and clicking heels sounded against the polished tiled floor as rapid-fire conversations echoed around the hallway to the sitting room. "I'm so sorry, Dario… yes, Frederico… okay, I'll get that over to you straight away."

I poured myself a scotch and sat down, staring out of the building. Talk of the wedding was the furthest thing on my fucking mind.

The ping of the elevator alerted me my house was free of strangers. Then the hellish sound of her heels clicked violently against the tiled floor, loud enough for me to know she was heading my way. "God! What the hell was that, Blake?"

"You tell me."

"You can't talk like that to these people. They are the best at what they do, and here you are, coming home like a cunt."

"You disrespected my father, Camille. What did you want me to say?"

"Okay, let's start again. Welcome home, fiancé." She smiled. Her perfectly made-up face made me even more tired, knowing the hours of effort that went into looking perfect.

She moved toward me.

"What are you doing, Camille?"

"I'm playing wifey." She came to sit on my lap, her lips on my neck.

"Get the fuck off me, Camille." I dug my hands into her hips and moved her off me.

"What the fuck, Blake?" She came to stand, smoothing down her mini-dress, then she flicked her hair out of her face.

"You expect me to want to ever sleep with you again after what you did?"

"Wake up," she said, throwing her leg off my lap. "This is New York, not Seatown."

"It's Seaview."

"Whatever. It's a small fucking town where people stay together for fifty years."

"And what's wrong with that?"

"I think you need to grow up and realize everyone fucks around. We are like the French. Men have mistresses, and women have their little fantasies. They keep us sane, and it keeps things alive. And this?" she said, arrowing her pointy finger between us. "This can work too if you want." She took a step closer to me. "Come on, baby. You know you can't resist me."

Oh, God. Bile lurched from my stomach to my throat. "That may have been true a long time ago when we'd just fuck. But as soon as you slept with whoever the fuck he was, that was it."

"Stop lying to yourself, Blake. You only ever fucked me to get your way to the top. You never loved me. No one has ever loved me."

"We had an arrangement, Camille, and I did care for you. At least before you fucked around."

"Cared?" She let out an exasperated sigh and threw her hands up to the sky. "Care, like an eighty-year-old in a nursing home?"

I took a swig of my scotch, and it burned down my throat. "Don't you think we both deserve more in life?"

She walked over to the window and looked down. "I think your dad dying has fucked you up."

I shook my head, staring at her back. "No, I'm serious."

"What are you talking about?" Turning around, she folded her hands across her chest, doubt playing on her lips.

"I don't hate you for what you did, but I think you are the lost daughter of an absent father and mother." I stood and moved to be beside her. "I think that's why you crave attention because you never had theirs."

She blinked a few times and rolled her chin down. *Was she about to cry?* I'd never seen her cry. When she looked back up, she was different.

"And I think you're a prick like my own dad… never home and thinks work is the most important thing there is."

I let out a sigh. "Camille. You knew this about me."

"Anyway, whatever. I have a boyfriend now. So let's just get married and be done with it."

I shook my head. Honestly, nothing surprised me about her. "Good for you."

"Really? So how was Lily, Lilu Lily, love of your life Lily?"

I laughed. She wasn't angry and didn't care. She was just dissimilar. "Well, since we're being honest. Lily was perfect."

"You always spoke about her like she was a queen. I'd hear you on the phone to your dad asking about her. Don't think I never heard that."

"Right."

"Well, jolly good shag then Down Under?"

"Oh God, Camille, don't try an Aussie accent, please!" She was being weirdly pleasant. It was strange and oddly refreshing. "So that doesn't bother you?"

She raised a perfect eyebrow. "You screwing around? No. Why would it?"

"Well, we are going to be married in less than four weeks. I find this whole arrangement so bizarre."

"You would, but this is normal in my world, Blake." She shook her head. "But that poor girl."

"Who?"

"Lily."

I slung back the rest of my scotch in one swift lug. It was a double, and it slid smoothly down the back of my throat.

"You've left her again, you asshole."

I know.

I was the biggest asshole on the planet. I'd done it again. But she'd known what she was getting into. She'd known all along I was only there for two weeks.

But as I stared at Camille, I knew I wanted to be with Lily. I wanted to touch her and kiss her again and feel the weightlessness I felt whenever I was around her. I bit my lip, not realizing the force had pierced my skin until I tasted the swirl of metallic blood in my mouth. I wiped my lip with the back of my hand and swallowed down the blood.

My phone pinged at the sound of an email, and I gravitated toward it. Picking it up, I noticed Camille was no longer there.

An email flashed on the screen with Robert's name and the heading, *Prenup, sign it.*

I poured myself another double. The prospect of marrying Camille was within my grasp. So was overseeing the firm's largest portfolio and the millions of dollars on the other end. All I had to do was sign the prenup and say *I do. I-fucking-do.*

Two words. What was so hard about that?

Fucking pussy.

20

LILY

The last of summer bloomed in the midday sky. The sun streamed down onto my untanned legs as I watched Amber frolic in the surf.

It was Saturday, the fourth one I'd spent in my new apartment. It wasn't like the cottage— peaceful and with a view like a postcard—but it was my new home. However, I'd been too busy working to even notice.

The lingering stench of mold plagued my room, the kitchen cupboard splintered, and the bathroom faucet pipes rattled in the wall. But I could be in the Burj Al Arab, and I still wouldn't be happy.

It had been nearly a month without him. Some days I had more pep in my step. In those days, I pushed him from my mind and focused on my floristry which I had taken up again. Then on the other days, the rain pelted down, and tears would fall freely. They burned like acid rain when I remembered what Blake and I had.

Amber was flat-out busy at work and couldn't help much. In the evenings, she came over to help unpack, and we'd get takeout and eat it on the floor. She was more useless than cotton candy to a diabetic, she was just that exhausted. But I welcomed the company, especially since she dragged me out every Friday for after-work drinks with her.

She was so similar to Blake, and it was scary—both slaving away and working countless hours, giving their lives to this concept of work I struggled to understand. But she was happy and didn't consider it to be work if she loved it. And that, I could understand.

Weeks turned into a month, and when I accepted Amber's offer to join her at the recently completed six-star Iluka Hotel, I took it.

"Can I get you some more champagne, miss?" A handsome man with smoothed hair and green eyes trailed my bikini-clad body before coming back to meet my gaze.

"Absolutely." I needed this drink more than anything right now. Anything to get my mind off this weekend. *Just the drink, friend.*

Foreign accents and beautiful people with thong bikinis and fat wallets surrounded us.

The law firm Amber worked for had organized a membership at the exclusive hotel. A perk for the employee of the month—which Amber had won for three out of the last six months.

Amber invited me to take my mind off Blake's impending nuptials this weekend. What better way to keep my mind off Blake than be surrounded by a smorgasbord of naked ripped chests and servers from exotic parts of the world? *If only it were that simple.*

Amber dove into the water and resurfaced under the midday sun. I wanted to throw myself in and get lost in the break, but this French champagne was too good to drink warm.

Couples surrounded me, rubbing lotion on one another and frolicking in the waves.

I'd gone and done it to myself again—I slept with him and became reattached. He was my everything. Why couldn't he see that?

"Here you are, miss." The server handed me the heavy flute, his gaze lingering longer this time down my body.

Jesus Christ, could he be so obvious.

"You might want to be more subtle next time." His eyes dragged to mine, and he looked at me wide-eyed. I shot him an accusatory eyebrow and a smile.

"Sorry, yes, miss." His face glowed red, matching my bikini, as he turned and walked away swiftly. The last thing he wanted to do was lose his job and his visa.

I sipped the champagne. The delicious bubbles danced on my tongue. I didn't want to celebrate anything, but it felt fitting. Letting go of Blake was something that needed to be done.

He was the only man I had ever loved, but his heart was in his work. His heart never could give love a chance. Maybe it once did. Maybe his mom leaving stripped him bare of believing in love at all.

Amber walked toward me, dripping under the sun. "Did you order me one?"

"No, sorry. I didn't know how long you were going to be. You might have to get it… I think I scared the server off."

"Oh, good one!" She tossed me a scowl and pulled a kaftan over her wet bikini.

I crossed and uncrossed my legs, unable to get comfortable as I watched her flirt with the bartender.

She returned with a huge smile and a glass of bubbles. "Cheers," she said, holding her glass up to mine.

I clinked my half-finished glass of bubbles with her. "What are we cheering to, exactly?"

She rolled her eyes. "My promotion, of course."

"Oh, of course." She'd told me all about her amazing promotion, and I couldn't have been more proud of her.

I swallowed down the refreshing alcohol.

"And to you, Lily, you go balls deep every time and seem to come out the other end, scars and all."

"Ain't that the truth." I took another big gulp before finishing the glass.

"You know, sometimes I wish I was more like you. Less emotional."

Amber laughed. "Don't wish for that."

"No, seriously. Look at you. So together all the time, the youngest in your office to get a promotion. You remind me so much of Blake. Maybe you two were meant for each other!"

"Hardly. I have no time for love." She tossed her wet brown hair over her shoulder. "But you do, Lil. You have all the time in the world. You designed your life like that, remember?"

She lowered her sunglasses and gave me a pointed stare.

"Yeah, freedom. It's all I ever wanted." Saying it aloud, I heard Blake's voice echo in my head. *You're still flapping about like you have zero responsibility, living day by day.*

I exhaled, staring at the end of the ocean. Maybe he was right. "Maybe it's time I knuckled down on something."

She slammed her glass down on the marble side table. "What? Since when?"

"I'm not saying work like you do. God, I could never do that. But maybe focus on a trade course in floristry rather than the community course I've been doing. I really feel like I've finally found my passion after trying everything else. Maybe I should consider it. Be a master of a trade instead of a jack of all trades and master of none."

"I think that's a brilliant idea."

"What will you do for money if you study?"

"I can still do my digital marketing work online, which earns me enough for now. And maybe after I finish the course, I can consider floristry full-time. Maybe even see if Seaview has a vacant shop, and I can start up my own thing."

"Well, holy shit. What have you done with my friend Lily?" she cried out in excitement.

She picked up her flute and was about to take a sip when she said, "Oh, by the way, I remembered where I'd heard the name Brennan before."

"Where?"

"His name came up in a meeting at work. Apparently, another law firm was suing him for defamation, amongst other things. The guy has a drug habit that could rival Keith Richards."

I blew out a puff of air. "Well, I'm glad that job's over, to be honest. I really don't want to see that creep again. I heard he got fired."

"Obviously, the good PR didn't do the trick." Amber laughed.

"Through no fault of his own. His drug habit was out of control, his secretary told me."

"His secretary?" Amber asked.

"Yes, we've become friends... well, online friends, at least. We're hoping to catch up next week for a coffee as she's coming down from the city to Seaview."

"Well, shit, don't go replacing me now with another bestie." She winked, but there was a truth to her voice I recognized.

"There's only one Amber," I acquiesced.

"Hell yeah, there is." She tossed me a wink as laughter rolled off our backs.

I settled back into my strappy deck chair, watching the ocean gurgle and purge. Children played in the sand or paddled in the tiny waves.

Amber got out her laptop. She was busier than she'd ever been with an extensive project coming up, so I let her be. I checked my phone. I don't know why. It wasn't like he'd called or texted me since leaving a month ago. Déjà-fucking-vu.

Closing my eyes, I listened to the ocean's soothing sound and felt the sun's warmth belt down on my skin.

I awoke to the sounds of kids shrilling in my ear. A little boy ran beside my chair throwing sand and missing his sister, scattering it all over my front instead.

"Wakey, wake," Amber said as she took me in. "You all right? You've been asleep for ages."

"What time is it?" I asked as I dusted myself off.

"Around three."

I straightened in the deck chair. "I had the strangest dream."

"What about?"

I clutched my forehead. "My parents."

I recalled the entire first few months. The day they died, then the days after, the feeling I relived it as though it was happening now. My hands trembled, and my skin popped with goose bumps. The night I lost them, the police came and took me to stay with protective services until they could locate a living relative. I felt numb, nothing. It wasn't until they sent me to my auntie a few days later that it hit, like an arrow shooting through the air and hitting the bullseye. I cried for days, weeks, and months. Until one day, I didn't have any more tears to shed. An ache brewed in my chest, and over time, it had lessened. In a way, I blamed them for leaving me. In a sick and twisted way, I felt abandoned by them. It wasn't their fault. None of it was. Accidents happened all the time, and this one took them from me too soon.

She closed the lid of her laptop and slid her Ray-Bans down the bridge of her nose.

A tear escaped from the corner of my eye, already wet from the dream. "Blake said I flap about, not committing to anything. Do you think it's possible I do all this stuff just so I can fill the void of them not being here?"

"Oh, hun." She reached out and placed her hand on my arm. "I think you only know the answer to that."

"Maybe I was the one who needed to feel the pain of my parents to forgive them."

She scrunched her brows together.

"I'll always love Blake, but this is about me. A multitude of other things can't fulfill the emptiness I've carried with me. I think that's what I've been doing all these years."

"What, art, yoga, Pilates, and now floristry?"

"Don't forget scuba diving. Yes, it's all been to fill a void."

"But your parents did not choose to leave you, Lil." She rested her hand on my arm.

"I know, but look at my pattern. The choices I've made. Yes, I love the freedom of it all, but I'm afraid of committing to one thing, and I think it's for fear of losing it."

"But you want to commit to Blake?" Amber asked.

I exhaled. "He was the only thing I wanted to commit to."

"So you know you can commit. It's not like you're immune to it. Narrow it down. If floristry is it, like you mentioned earlier, focus on that for the year and see where it takes you."

I nodded. It was as though a cloud had lifted. It wouldn't bring Blake back to me, but it was a little piece of the puzzle I could control.

"One-year floristry course, here we come."

I looked at the cave in the distance. The cave where Blake had kissed me like he loved me and held me as though I was the only woman in the world.

I nodded to myself.

I wish you well, Blake. We will always have our memories, but you are where you belong.

21

BLAKE

T aking a break from work on the eve of my wedding seemed like the normal thing to do. Yet, there was nothing normal about the arrangement I was walking into headfirst. Tensions were high in the office with Robert's asshole behavior fast becoming the norm. He wasn't just an ass to me, either. Anyone that crossed his path was in the firing line.

He'd insisted I sign the prenup weeks ago, but I delayed, piling on excuse after excuse. The latest excuse was my lawyer's workload was holding it up.

When I announced I was stepping out of the office to fetch a coffee, my team looked at me like I'd grown a pair of tits overnight.

Fuck them.

Disregarding them, I walked block after block, ignoring the dings coming through on my phone. After a while, I'd rounded the corner, arriving at Bryant Park. The warm air reminded me of endless sunny beach days and the chime of an ice cream truck, the only pull to take us away from the surf.

I sat on the park bench, watching kids play hopscotch and

taking turns sliding down the forest green slide. Without a care in the world, they twirled and giggled, their ribbons swirling in the air as moms chatted nearby. I was jealous.

Once upon a time, I possessed that level of freedom. It was just her and I against the world. Her smile was the best part of my day. Nothing else mattered as much as she did. Until I had to go and fuck it all up.

Again, my phone vibrated in my suit pants pocket, and I dug to pull it out. *Fuck.* The prenup wasn't the only thing I hadn't signed. The realtor for Dad's house in Seaview had a buyer, and all they needed was my signature. Lily signed yesterday. She said she would move on the day I left, and true to her word, she was doing just that.

Pain stabbed me in the chest like a blunt ice pick. I sighed. Not now. I clicked the call sending it to voicemail and slid the phone back into my pocket. It was painfully obvious Lily was done with not only the house but me as well. She had signed the papers and hadn't called me since I left.

What the fuck did I expect?

I don't know why, but my pen couldn't touch the contract. I needed more time. Parting with the house was like parting with Lily and my life in Seaview forever. *But hadn't I made that decision for both of us when I got on the plane?*

Fuck, I was getting married tomorrow. It wasn't like I was getting out of that one, either.

I hadn't realized I was walking again until I stopped abruptly at a hotdog stall. *Oh well, why not?* My trainer had been busting my ass ever since I'd returned. What he didn't know wouldn't kill him.

"What can I get you, sir?"

"Cheese, onions, chili sauce… actually, give me the works."

"Rough day, hey?" The short man with a friendly face threw me a worry-free smile.

"Rough month." I gave him a lopsided smile.

"You know, my papa would say don't sweat the small stuff."

"My dad died recently," I blurted out, oddly confiding in the stranger on a corner stand.

"I'm sorry, my friend. That must be very hard."

I cleared my throat. "Thank you."

Meticulously, he sprinkled shredded cheese and onions on the hot dog, methodically covering every inch evenly and taking the utmost pride in his job. "Was he a wise man?"

I nodded. "He was. A wise and proud man." Suddenly, overwhelmed by an emotion that came out of nowhere, I fumbled for a bill in my wallet. Like Dad, you could tell this man shared the same amount of pride, just like my old man and his handyman skills. Their dedication and commitment, hands down, outweighed most of my team, and they earned a fraction of their salary.

I handed over a fifty and took the hotdog from his hands. "Thanks for listening."

"Hey, man, your change," he yelled after me, but I had already walked away.

"Keep it." I kept walking, unable to comprehend the over-whelming feeling of loss that threatened to take hold.

I shook my head and set a fast pace, rounding the corner toward my office.

"Blake?" A voice cornered me from behind. "I thought that was you."

I turned around. *Oh, God.* "Jazzie, hi."

She glared at me like the asshole I was.

"How is she?" I asked, needing to know if she was suffering as much as me. *Fuck. I couldn't help it.*

She looked at me with wide eyes. "Now, there's a question."

I put my hand on my temples, the pads of my fingers digging into my skin. "Can we talk?" I asked.

"I'm just on my way to the gallery. But I guess I can spare a few minutes, although…" She tilted her chin down, giving me the once over.

"Jazzie, please," I pleaded.

She held her hands up. "All right, all right."

I tossed my hotdog into the nearest trash bin.

"No good?"

"Nah, don't need it. How's Kit doing?" I asked, falling into step beside her.

"He's great. Just finishing up the album, then he'll be on tour soon."

"I like his new stuff. It's a different vibe," I admitted truthfully.

"Well, he has a sweet muse as inspiration." She grinned, then it tipped into a hard smile. "Anyway, let's cut the chit-chat." She turned onto East 51st Street, and I followed. She walked toward the front of an office building and sat down far enough away from others. "So, you're getting married tomorrow."

I sat next to her, gripping the wooden slats until my knuckles couldn't stretch anymore. "You've heard, huh?"

"It's kind of everywhere, Blake. And Lily is my best friend. In fact, she'd kill me if she knew I was talking to you."

"I bet she would." I stared distantly as the soft curves of her face and her bright blue eyes came into my mind.

"Blake?"

I snapped out of it. "Yes. Robert's media team has been spreading the word of our nuptials for weeks."

Heck, the guest list alone would rival the net worth of a small country.

"You sound thrilled," she joked.

"Look, it is what it is. It's just good business."

"It's absurd," she spat out.

"Thanks."

"Come on, Blake. Is this what you want me to talk about? Your fake wedding?"

"No, of course not. How is she, Jazzie?"

"So you haven't called her again?"

I shook my head, disgusted with myself.

"Déjà vu."

"Well, this time, I suppose it's different. I'm getting married tomorrow."

"I don't think it's different at all. Feelings are just that, feelings." She shook her head. "Look, Lily is and always will be okay. She is resilient. She picks herself up and dusts herself off. Since that tragic accident that took her parents, she's had to fend for herself. She might wear her heart on her sleeve, but when that backfires, she picks herself up again. Especially when the love of her life pushes her away for the second time."

"She said I was the love of her life?" Hope bloomed in my chest.

"If you want to know how she is, you can pick up the damn phone. I think you *need* to know how she is. I think you miss her like air."

I put my head in my hands. "Of course I do."

"Well, do something about it. It's not too late. You're not married. You haven't signed your life away to the devil, Robert Jackson himself."

I widened my eyes. "How do you know about that?"

"Women talk."

Ain't that the truth. There might be nearly two million people living in Manhattan, but that didn't stop women and their circles from reaching other women and their circles.

"What am I supposed to do, Jazzie? I've worked my entire life to get here. This arrangement sets me up for life, and to risk all that on a girl?"

"You've got it all wrong, Blake. Lily isn't just any girl, and you know it."

My heart thundered, and my neck heated. I couldn't sit still on the bench any longer, so I stood. "Thanks for speaking with me, Jazzie."

"By the way, I think you got in her ear about committing to something," she said, standing.

"What do you mean?"

"She's committed to her floristry studies. She's finishing up her community college course this weekend actually and signed up for a year-long course. She's even talking about opening up a florist shop one day."

A wide smile fell on my mouth. "She'd be so amazing at that."

Jazzie glanced at me sideways. "So I guess I have you to thank for that."

"I guess. Maybe I'm not that bad, after all?" I rubbed my chin, hoping that one day they could all forgive me.

"No, you are," she deadpanned.

Her phone buzzed, and she slid it out of her handbag. "Kit's calling. I got to go." Her face lit up at the mere sight of his name.

I knew that feeling, but I'd convinced myself it wasn't real and wouldn't last. I'd buried it since Mom walked out on us.

* * *

Downstairs, the flurry of photographers and people on the guest list gathered. Politicians, celebrities, and financial king-pins of Manhattan all graced the ballroom. I'd gone down an hour earlier, unable to sit still. Different varieties of orchids hung from the ceiling, flown in from Singapore. Camille had wanted them, and the only reason I knew was because Robert went on a rampage in the office after seeing the bill. I'd avoided Camille since being back, which was fine with her.

And her boyfriend.

We occupied the entire floor of the Plaza, my suite at one end and Camille's at the other. I walked out my door, down the carpeted hallway, and snuck into her room, finding a seat in the front room and away from her team of people surrounding her.

I slid my hand back and forth on the tan leather armchair. She was yet to notice me on the Chesterfield in the front room. But I could see her admiring herself in front of the mirror. It was only a matter of time. Everything had boiled down to this one moment—a decision to marry Camille and have the future and certainty I always wanted. Marrying into one of the most prestigious families in Manhattan was everything. Top of the list.

I toiled, hustled, and spent every single moment trying to get where I wanted to be. I even imagined it every night before I closed my eyes. I saw myself in the mansion with the sports cars and house in the Hamptons, and I was at the precipice of having it all. All I had to do was jump.

But there was a reason I couldn't sleep last night and the countless nights before that. I was a coward. I'd been lying to myself this entire time. Everything I had ever wanted didn't matter if it wasn't with her.

Camille drained the color from my rainbow, and since returning from Seaview, my life was blander than dry toast. Only Lily could paint my world, and it vanished when I walked away from her for the second time.

She confessed that she loved me, and even then, I chose this life over her. A life of certainty and a loveless marriage. A lie, which led me to being here.

I didn't know if there was any hope for Lily and me, but I sure as hell knew what I didn't want, and that was Camille. I couldn't let a family dictate who or what I could do with my life. I sure as fuck hadn't gotten to where I was today by bending over. I achieved it with hard work, steely grit, and fortitude, and I'd be damned if I was going to lay down and take it up the ass now.

But none of it mattered. I would rather be in the orchard, in the cottage, or lying in the tent under the starlight with Lily than here. It wasn't a burning friendship that I could squash. It wasn't a one-night stand when I took her virginity. I could pretend she was nothing when she was my everything.

Camille saw me in the mirror, and her eyes widened. A moment later, she'd excused herself from her team and slid inside the front room. Her ivory dress was covered with lace and beading, and she looked stunning.

"Blake, you know you can't be here," she whisper-shouted.

"Shh, Camille, sit down for a minute." The last thing I wanted was for her bridesmaids and makeup team to come rushing in behind her before I had a chance to say what I needed to say.

"But we're going down now."

I closed the door behind her and walked around her large skirt, careful not to step on it. She looked pretty, but she wasn't the girl for me.

"Why did you close the door? Blake, what the hell's going on?"

"Just two minutes. Please, for me." I flashed her my sweetest smile.

"I can't sit in this, Blake."

We stared at each other, and I thought about how delicately I could make my delivery.

Oh fuck it, she has an actual boyfriend, for fuck's sake.

"Camille, this isn't going to happen."

She counters almost immediately. "Oh yes, it is. Do you know who's down there?"

I shook my head from side to side. "I don't care."

She waved her arms around. "Tell me, is this because of Lily?"

"No." *Not entirely.*

"But Daddy promised you millions if you married me and more if we got pregnant. We can still live our separate lives."

"You don't want me, Camille. You never have, and the truth is I've never loved you."

She closed her eyes briefly, bringing her hands to her face and shielding her eyes from me.

Oh shit. Too far? I was breaking up with her on our wedding day, but was it a breakup if we weren't really together to begin with?

I leaned in, placing one arm around her shoulders. She gripped the lapels of my Tom Ford Jacket, sniffing. *Was she crying?*

I released her hug, and she stared at me only a whisper away. Her eyes were glossy.

"Are you crying?"

"Not over you, you loser." Out of the corner of my eye, I saw her hand flicker, and the next thing I knew, a blinding sting throbbed along my cheekbone. "Take that, you asshole."

"Jesus, Camille!" My hand flew up to my cheek, the sharp sting reverberating down to my jaw.

She ran out of the room, and I was grateful for her swift exit.

Now all I had to do now was get the fuck out without being seen.

I rubbed my cheek along the hallway and back to my suite.

I guess I deserved that. Camille would be perfectly fine. Robert would marry her off to someone else, and she would blissfully live in and out of rehab. Although I hoped her life wouldn't end up that way.

After gathering the last of my things from the bedroom, I picked up my suitcase and set it against the front door.

Relief flooded me. Uncertainty plagued me, but for once, I couldn't care less. Now I knew why Lily craved it so much. The feeling of freedom was like nothing I'd ever felt before in my life. But I had one hurdle left, and he was due any second.

I had a plan. Although loose, it would have to do for now. I wouldn't give up my job. I'd just put it on pause. But explaining that to Robert could go one of two ways. I knew which way it would go, and I didn't care. He was just another obstacle on my way to freedom, a kink in the chain to getting closer to Lily.

My phone rang, and I slipped it out of my pocket.

"Roger."

"Blake, finally, I've got you!" Roger let out a sigh of relief. "I need those signed contracts for the house to sell urgently, please."

"I can't sell it."

"What?"

"I'll explain it all to you in forty-eight hours. I'm flying home."

"No, Blake, please."

The door flung open, and Robert entered in his tuxedo. "Got to go, Roger."

"Wai—"

I clicked off the call.

Shit, I felt like breaking up with him would be harder than Camille. Now that should tell me something right then and there.

He took me in. I'd loosened my tie and unbuttoned the first two buttons of my Tom Ford shirt.

"Why aren't you ready?"

"Have you spoken to Camille, Robert?"

"Of course not. I've been downstairs with the guests. I'm assuming you've got the prenup here for me?"

I flopped on the armchair. "I don't want to sign the prenup, Rob."

"What do you want? More money? They always want to

extort at the last hour." He paced up and down the entranceway of the suite.

"No, I don't want your money. And do you really think you can sell your daughter off?"

"I can do whatever I want," he snapped.

"Sure you can. But based on that rationale, why can't I?" He stopped pacing and glared at me.

"What are you playing at?"

"I'm not marrying Camille, Robert." His sullen cheeks glowed crimson. "Because she isn't the one for me."

He laughed. "And who are you saving yourself for?"

"Lily… if she'll have me."

"Who the fuck is Lily?" he snapped.

"She is my neighbor in Seaview."

"Come on, did Fred put you up to this? You sound like you need to be committed."

"Why? Because I'm in love?"

He planted his legs wide, his nostrils flaring. "Stop being a pussy. Come on. Everyone is out there. You're not doing this. This is career suicide. You can kiss your entire career goodbye."

"I know it is. And I thought you'd say that."

"And?"

"And the reason you want me to marry your daughter and keep me on a leash like her is because I'm shit-hot at what I do."

"Don't go giving yourself a blow job now."

"You know it. I've made you millions. Hundreds of millions with the investments I've brought on board. So I don't care if you let me go, I'm leaving anyway."

"What, and go back to Australia?"

"Yeah, why not?"

"All for one girl?"

"She's not just one girl." I couldn't help but smile widely.

"Jesus fuck, are you listening to yourself? I knew I should have gone with the son of an oil magnate. At least then he would be man enough to marry her." His face bloomed brighter by the second as tiny beads of sweat appeared on his forehead

"If you think marrying for money is manning up, then you've got your priorities wrong."

"You're telling me…" He stepped forward, wielding his arm in readiness to clock me, but the old man was so slow I could see it coming from a mile away.

"Robert, stop. You'll give yourself a heart attack." He launched at me, and I bent his arm behind him and pinned him against the wall.

"Get the fuck off me. Security!" he spat out, fuming.

I released him. "Call your dog squad off. I'm gone anyway."

"Fuck you, Blake." He clutched at his arm and slid down the wall. Seriously, the old man should step foot in a gym sometime instead of being holed up in the office.

I shouldered out of my jacket and threw it over my shoulder. Something fell out, landing on my shiny Italian shoes. An envelope with Dad's handwriting stared back at me. I blinked, trying to understand what I was looking at.

The letter from Dad's lawyer. When he read the will, he'd handed it to me. I'd tucked it away in this jacket, the same jacket I'd worn to Dad's funeral. With everything going on, I'd completely forgotten about it. Quickly, I scooped it up and gripped it with my hand holding the jacket while wheeling my suitcase out with the other.

"You can't do this, Blake," Rob yelled after me.

"Like you, I can do whatever the fuck I want."

* * *

Running out of the hotel's back exit didn't buy me much time. It took less than an hour for the news to leak that I'd bailed at my own wedding.

Likely planned and completely orchestrated by the devil himself, Robert's media team swung straight into action. Spinning the story in a way that he and his daughter appeared the victims in all this.

He painted me as the villain—the skirt-chaser taking advantage of his innocent daughter. But the problem was, the papers had already photographed her with other men long before I walked out on her, so I knew the story wouldn't stick. *And even if it did…*

"Can I get you a drink before takeoff?" The flight attendant asked as she held her tray of bubbles and little bottles of spirits.

"No, thank you," I said, returning my gaze to the tarmac.

"Are you sure?" She smiled, a flirty undertone to her question.

"I'm sure." I threw her a shaded smile, and she turned around with heat in her step.

Right. I clearly needed a plan.

I wanted Lily. And I fucked it all up. How to fix this.

She made it clear that if I walked away, we were done. She wouldn't think of me ever again. The thought stole the air from my lungs, replacing it with sand.

Fuck! I rubbed my throbbing temples. What was I even doing if I didn't stand a chance?

There was always a chance.

The plane ascended, and I took out the smudged and dirty envelope I'd had in my possession for over a month. I shook my head, unable to understand how I could forget about something so precious. Guilt washed over me. But as I tore it open, something or someone spoke to me because the timing couldn't have been more perfect.

.   .   .

Son,

You're probably wondering why I chose Brennan to leave the house to.

I have always been a bit of a joker, a larrikin. But deep down, I was so much more than that.

Blake, I know you didn't want to be anything like me. And that was okay. I even wanted that for you. I didn't want you to suffer, but I didn't want you ending up like those snotty-nosed Grammar boys you grew up with, either. You wanted everything that Brennan had. I had never seen anyone go after something with the blinding tenacity you did. And that's great, but in the entire scheme of things, it's not everything, son.

Your mother leaving me mattered. It mattered to you as much as it did me. I see that. I watched you with Lily. You two couldn't have been more right for one another if there was a matchmaking show with just you two on it.

I needed to put you two together for a short time for you to see that there was love there. All those years ago, when you left her, you left yourself too. Don't be afraid of love just because it left me heartbroken. I would rather have been hurt by your mother than not have had her to love at all.

And Brennan? Brennan was the anchor to keep you in Seaview. Because I knew you wouldn't have stayed for the money alone or for Lily, but throw him into the mix and come hell or high water, you would do everything in your power not to give that asshole a dime.

I've lived the best life I knew how. I don't regret a thing. I want that for you. A rich, full life. Rich with happiness and love. And you, son, deserve all those things. You brought so much joy into my life.

I love you.

Dad.

PS. If you get rid of the truck or the lathe, I will come back from the dead and bury you.

A chuckle rolled over my shoulders as I wiped away a tear.

22

LILY

Never had I wanted to slap down Amber and Jazzie more than right now. *Why did I say yes?* Samuel was good-looking with big brown eyes, a shaved head, and quite tall. Otherwise, Amber wouldn't have swiped right to accept. Amber and Jazzie worked like Thelma and Louise in cahoots, setting me up with an online dating profile. I didn't want any part of it, so they found a photo and wrote my profile without telling me.

The two of them thought it would be the ideal way to get over Blake. They didn't want me moping about and feeling sorry for myself. Sure, in theory, it made sense, but heck, a date was the furthest thing from my mind. Especially since a select few from my floristry class and I were knee-deep in preparations for our very first wedding tomorrow.

Best way to get over someone is to get under someone. Thanks, Amber. That didn't change the fact that Blake was getting married in less than twenty-four hours.

"So tell me about yourself. You know all about me now," Samuel inquired, taking a sip of his almond latte.

Do I? There was some mention of a German Shepard

named Sandy, a job as a teacher, or did he say a preacher? *Oh, dear.*

I really wish I'd said no, but Amber had worn me down day after day, nagging me to go on a date. And day after day, I'd said no until she got me at a weak moment, and I said yes just to shut her up. I had completely forgotten about the date until she mentioned it while we were sipping champagne beachside yesterday.

I picked at my Bircher muesli. "Well, you name it, I've probably done it."

He smiled, wanting to know more.

"I've been an artist, Pilates instructor, learned the pottery wheel, tried scuba diving and yoga." I picked at the pepitas, scooping them out and to the side of my plate. "Now I'm studying floristry, and to pay the bills, I'm a freelance online marketer. That's me in a nutshell."

"And you don't like pepitas?"

I chuckled. "No."

"Wow, so you have done it all. Why so much?"

I laughed uncontrollably from the depths of my belly.

He scrunched his perfect eyebrows into a line. "Did I miss something?"

I regained my composure, then took a big sip of peppermint tea. "No, Samuel. You asked why. Let me tell you."

I leaned back in my chair. "Well, first, my parents died in a tragic accident when I was fifteen—"

"I'm so sorry."

"Anyway, when they died, they left me with a terrible feeling of abandonment. Except I hadn't realized that until recently. And if that wasn't enough, my neighbor, Blake, who I grew up with, took my virginity… sorry if that's too much information… before leaving me in the middle of the night to fly to New York and never talk to me again. That was until last month when he came back because his dad died. Then we were stuck together for two weeks because we had to renovate his dad's house in order to sell it. That's when I fell in love with him all over again. And like good old Blake, he left me *again*. But this time to get married to a cheating socialite who doesn't deserve him. Oh, and that day is today. So answering your question, I did all that stuff to fill a void that fucked me up years ago." I exhaled, feeling better. "But I'm okay now. I've moved on."

With wide eyes, he stared, probably thinking I belonged in Seaview's finest asylum.

* * *

Yesterday's date was an epic fail. Samuel made a swift exit after my verbal yet cathartic explosion, and I didn't try to stop him. Dating was a terrible idea, although I couldn't blame Amber and Jazzie for trying.

Monday morning hit like a migraine. I promised myself no more tears, but they sprang like a waterfall.

I promised myself I wouldn't look at the tabloids. I couldn't for fear of truly spiraling down the rabbit hole with no way back. I turned off my phone and didn't check my socials, instead choosing to arrive at the pavilion by the beach before everyone else in my class to get a jump on the busy day ahead.

My teacher, Katie, pulled into the parking lot. Shutting the door, she spotted me walking toward her, lowering her glasses just to make sure. "I thought I was the only one who got up this early."

"And miss all this?" My gaze hovered toward the breathtaking sunrise dancing across the edge of the ocean. "It's the best part of the day. Plus, I've got about four hundred roses to wire in eight hours."

"Good point."

Katie was a retired florist who taught the community

course for anyone wanting to try their hand at floristry without the full-time commitment. Occasionally, students were given the opportunity to work on a wedding. It was a win for us as we got practical on-the-job experience while the bride and groom received arrangements at wholesale prices. I was starting the trade course next week, but there was no way I'd pass up on the opportunity, especially since Katie volunteered me for the main piece—the archway where the bride and groom would exchange their vows.

"Come on. Let me help you get started." She unlocked the padlock and slid down the metal chain that held the two wooden doors together.

The aromas of sweet jasmine and roses hit me like a flower punch as soon as the doors swung open. "Wow." As well as jasmine, white roses, lisianthuses, cream hydrangeas, and baby's breath overflowed in the temporary white buckets that housed them. Empty vases, ribbon reels, and a multitude of pins, wire, and secateurs were scattered across the wooden tables. And in the corner, the enormous curved wire archway stood bare, waiting for a covering of roses and forest greens.

Time had seriously flown, and my neck was ramrod stiff from placing a gazillion roses in the archway. I cranked my neck up and around in a circular motion, trying to get some blood flow back into it.

"Lily, that looks phenomenal." Alison placed a cup of peppermint tea on the table beside me and marveled at my creation. She had finished the bride's bouquet some time ago and was wandering between the students, ensuring we were all fed and watered.

"Last one!" I cried out in exhaustion. Wrapping it around the thin wire, I delicately placed it into the one tiny gap that remained.

I wiped my forehead with the back of my hand and took a

step back to admire my work. *Whoa.* The archways teemed with bursting roses, forest greens, and delicate silver foliage.

"Simply stunning, Lily," Katie said.

I turned around. Katie and the rest of the students were behind me, watching. *How long had they been watching?*

Katie turned to the other students. "Jay, Millie, Amelia... now, that is what I call a florist in flow."

I laughed. "Thanks, Katie. Not a florist yet, but hopefully, one day." But the more I thought about a career with flowers, the more I was certain this was the right path for me.

"Hun, the only way you won't be a florist is if you give up."

I smiled. *Well, that's not happening.*

"Now, come on, let's take a well-deserved break before we set up."

The help rarely hung back to watch the wedding. After all, denim shorts and a Ramones vintage T-shirt didn't quite fit the dress code. But Alison and I stayed. Her kids were grown up and left the nest, and her husband was playing bridge, so she didn't need to be anywhere. And why I insisted on staying? Who knew? Probably because I wanted to torture myself some more by being at a goddamn wedding.

The wind swirled along the beachfront as the bride descended the sandy aisle to meet her groom, the sun setting behind them. I watched the groom's reaction while everyone watched the bride. He puffed out his chest and smiled with his eyes. He was so proud to be marrying the love of his life, and when she met him under the archway, the way they looked at each other made my heart burst open.

"Ladies and Gentlemen, we are gathered here today to celebrate the love Dylan and Mia have for one another."

"Look how stunning your work is," Alison whispered.

"I just hope it doesn't get blown over in this wind," I whispered back.

Another swirling breeze hit the shoreline, and I wrapped my arms around my body, shielding it from the cold.

I felt a warm jacket on my shoulders, and I pulled it up. I turned to Alison to thank her, but she just stared ahead.

I felt the soft fabric between my fingers, wondering where the hell it came from.

"You look cold," a voice sounded from behind, and my shoulders went tight.

I turned around and suddenly went ice cold. Brennan stood behind me, his eyes bloodshot and puffy. He looked like he hadn't slept in days.

"What are you doing here, Brennan?"

"I'm a friend of the groom." He leaned in so his breath was on my neck, and he wrapped his hands around my stomach. "And I missed you."

I jerked away. "Get off me." My voice came out in a shrill.

"Shh." A few people from the back row turned around and stared.

I turned back to Brennan, his pupils dilated. *Was he high?*

"I think we have something, Lily. We always have."

Nausea plagued me. "Are you high?"

"Lily, are you okay?" Alison scowled at Brennan, then sided up to me.

"No, I'm not. Brennan, just go before you ruin this wedding."

"Come on, baby, you and me. You've always wanted me." He reached for my hand, and I slapped it away.

"Don't touch me, Brennan," I cried out through gritted teeth. The mere presence of him made my skin crawl.

"You heard the lady. Now I think you should please leave," Alison said, standing firmly beside me.

"Who are you, her mom? No, wait, your parents are dead, right?"

I recoiled at his words, tingles of discomfort bursting all over my skin.

"Right, what's going on here?"

It took me a moment to register there was another man next to us. I glanced up to find the groom's dad looking between us.

Shit.

"I'm sorry, but this man is harassing me," I said apologetically.

"Oh please, she wants it," Brennan snapped.

Now, I realized the officiant had stopped the ceremony. The bride, groom, and wedding guests had turned around, and all eyes were on me. My face flushed the color of an overripe tomato.

"Brennan, what the fuck are you doing here?"

Out of nowhere, a blistering punch landed on Brennan's face.

Gasps from the guests swirled on the breeze as Alison pulled me away from the commotion unfolding before our eyes.

Brennan clutched his jaw. "Fuck you, Dylan!" he screamed as blood sprayed onto the pavement.

"That's for Mia. Now get the fuck out of here before I call the cops."

He crawled off the ground, clutching his leg, and barely regained his balance. He wiped his nose and flicked off the blood before taking a long look between the groom and me.

The groom stepped forward. "Don't make me, Brennan. You know I will."

He let out a loud sigh and turned around. We watched him limp across the road, and when he was out of sight, the groom turned to me. "Are you okay?"

"Yes, I'm so sorry about all of this."

"Don't be sorry, the guy's a jerk, harassed my fiancé for over a year, and we had to get a restraining order against him."

"What?" I clasped my hands around my mouth.

The bride came and rushed to his side. "Babe, are you okay?" She put her hand up to his cheek, then rubbed her hand across his bruise in a moment of affection.

"I'm fine," he said, reassuring her. Once she was satisfied, she turned to me.

"Sorry about Brennan. I don't think we've met. I'm Mia."

"Hi, I'm Lily," I replied in the worst timing of introductions ever.

"She did your archway," Alison interjected.

"Really? Oh my God, it is so beautiful. Thank you so much."

"I'm so happy you like it." I looked around, forgetting we had an audience.

The groom circled his hand into his fiancé's. "If you don't mind, I want to marry this girl before she changes her mind."

They smiled at one another, and something tugged inside my chest.

"Not a chance," she whispered loud enough for me to hear.

With Brennan out of the picture, the bride and groom got on with saying their I dos, and the officiant promptly announced them, husband and wife. They kissed each other under the flowering archway and picture-perfect backdrop of the deep blue ocean.

* * *

"Lil, where have you been? I've been trying to get a hold of you."

"I'm just about to get on the bus. Sorry, I only just switched my phone back on. You won't believe who I bumped into, Amber. Hello… Amber?"

"Yes, sorry."

"Brennan was at the wedding. The sleaze bag tried hitting on me again, and the groom punched his lights out. Turns out, he was harassing the groom's fiancé."

"Well, I guess he had it coming. Hey, listen, you should swing past your old place. When I passed it earlier on my way home, loads of debris and branches littered the property."

"Oh shit. Is there any damage?" Quickly, I crossed the road, signaling the bus up ahead.

"I couldn't see, it may have clipped the back cottage, but I can't be sure."

"Okay, I'm just getting on the bus now. I'll stop by. Hopefully, it's just a big mess and no serious damage."

"Let me know how you go."

It only took five minutes on the bus to reach Al's old house. I walked from the bus stop toward the house at the end of the street.

What happens if the property is damaged? I'd have to arrange repairs, wouldn't I? I'd never been in this situation before. I could call the agent. He would know what to do.

As I approached the house, I craned my neck, trying to get a glimpse of the rooftop and the damage and debris Amber spoke about. But from the ambient street lighting, it was too difficult to see.

I stood outside the home. Everything looked intact except for a turned-over pot and debris on the ground. I rounded the corner. A warm glow from within the cottage lit up the grounds around it. Damn, I must have left the light on weeks ago when I moved out.

When I opened the side gate, it creaked nostalgically. I scanned the backyard but saw nothing unusual. No branches, a bit of debris, but nothing out of the ordinary.

Stepping on the pebbled pathway, I walked toward the front door of the cottage just to make sure. I pulled out my key and put it in the barrel, turning it. But it was already unlocked.

Fear plagued me. What if Brennan hadn't gone home and was waiting for me here? He was too big and too strong to fight on my own.

I quickly pulled my key out, turned around, and proceeded to tiptoe back toward the gate. *Shit, the gate!* He would have heard me open it.

"Lily, stop."

Mid-step, I stopped and turned around. "Blake, what the hell are you doing here? You almost gave me a heart attack." I clutched at my chest, expelling a breath I hadn't realized I was holding.

"Are you all right?" He walked toward me, a worried look peeling onto his face.

"Yes. I am now. I thought you were Brennan."

I'm relieved you're not. But what the fuck are you doing here?

"Why would Brennan be here?" His hand pulled at his hair as his jaw ticked.

"Would you just chill, Blake? He was at this wedding I did the flowers for, and he was harassing me. I thought he had followed me back here."

He sheathed his teeth in rage. "That asshole, I'll fucking kill him!"

I put my hands up, exhausted from the day and confused to see Blake on my old doorstep. "Just stop, Blake. What are you doing here?"

"I came for you, Lily." He gave me a nervous smile, and I shut him down immediately.

"No, you didn't." I walked straight past him and into my old kitchen. I turned to pull the door behind me when his hand touched mine. I immediately withdrew it, pushing away the tingles of warmth and familiarity that flooded my veins.

"Lily, please... just hear me out."

"No. You should just get back on your plane and go back to Camille."

"I don't want to." He looked down at me, forcing me to glance up at him. *No, he's not going to suck me in again with those hypnotic greens.*

"I don't care what you want." I walked around the kitchen counter, hoping the solid gap between us would help my resolve.

"I've come all this way. Will you just hear me out?"

"Just say what you have to say, then leave."

He paused as if trying to find the right words, and my gaze flicked to his wedding finger. But there was no ring. Wasn't he married? *Fuck, it made no difference.* I couldn't help but be curious, despite his awkwardness.

"I… ah…" He ran his hand through his sandy hair.

"Blake. What are you here for? You could have signed the realtor papers from New York."

"Just give me a minute, please," he pleaded as he paced back and forth in the tiny cottage.

I took him in. Stiff shoulders and sudden movements. Beady brows and flushed skin. This wasn't the confident Blake I knew. I'd never seen him this rattled before. I leaned against the kitchen counter and waited for what felt like an eternity.

He walked around the bench but stopped short of touching me. "I can't do this anymore."

"Good, neither can I. That's what I've been trying—"

"No, that's not what I meant. I can't lie to myself anymore." He shook his head, and his gaze rolled up to meet mine. He grabbed both my hands and took them in his.

"I fucking love you, Lily. I always have. I was just too blind to see that something so perfect was right in front of me this entire time."

222

I gripped the countertop for support as a thousand butterflies swarmed inside my stomach.

"The night I left you to leave Seaview was the hardest decision I've ever had to make. I couldn't wait till morning to say goodbye because I wouldn't have left. Looking into your eyes, I couldn't have possibly left you. I chose my career then, but I choose you now."

"Now?" I inhaled a shaky breath. "How do I know you won't put me second ever again? I might be resilient, Blake, but I'm not unbreakable."

His thumb caressed my hand. "I quit my job, Lil. You mean more to me than any career." His eyes radiated with an honesty I'd never seen before.

A light-hearted feeling started building in my chest. I turned away from him, trying to take in everything he'd just said. I couldn't look him in the eyes for fear of losing my own composure. "It's not enough, Blake."

"I'm begging you, Lil. I've been a dick."

I turned around and nodded. "A monster dick."

"Monster dick, yes." He grinned.

"That's not what I meant!" I shoved him in the chest, but he didn't budge. I was powerless to stop the smirk from spreading into my cheeks.

He leaned closer so his breath was on my cheek. "Give me one more chance, Lily. I want to make a life with you here. Nothing makes sense in my life without you." He stroked my cheek with the back of his hand, and I closed my eyes, absorbing his touch. When I opened them, he tilted my face to his. "You are and always will be my number one."

Since the very first night we made love six long years ago, I'd been waiting to hear him say those three words. My head told me to send him packing. My heart thumped in my rib cage, swiping the breath from my lungs.

I didn't know what the future held, but one thing I knew for certain was that my gut never lied. A smile spread into my cheeks. "You, Blake, will be the death of me."

He bowed his head. "Shit, Lily, I honestly didn't know which way that was going to go." His hand circled my waist, and he pulled me into his chest. "Come here, beautiful."

I stood on my tiptoes and gazed up into his eyes. His warm breath tickled my face, and in one swift motion, his lips crashed down onto mine in a kiss that made me weak at the knees.

After a beat, he pulled away and whispered in my ear, "I knew you wanted to make out with me."

W e'd fumbled with each other in the sheets of her cottage all night and twice that morning.

If words could describe the feeling of her giving me another chance, I would try. But there weren't any that could describe the feeling I had.

"Hey, sexy. What are you thinking about?" Lily asked as she stroked my chest hairs. *Fuck, I loved it when she did that.*

"Just that forty-eight hours ago, my life was going in a direction it shouldn't have been."

"How's Camille?" She turned on her side, propping herself up with her elbow.

"Are you seriously asking?"

"Well, yes and no." She smiled, her blonde hair all tousled and wayward from our lovemaking.

"From the slap she gave me when I told her I didn't want to marry her, my guess is she was upset for all of two minutes. Upset because of the humiliation, nothing else."

"Are you okay?" she asked, with a genuine sincerity only my Lily could have.

"I'm perfect." I ran a finger across her lower lips, and she shivered at the touch.

"And what about your job? It meant so much to you."

I stroked her cheek. "You mean more."

"Oh, say it again. I don't think I'll ever get tired of you putting me first!" I slapped him on the chest playfully.

"You mean so much more, Lily. I fucking love you. I'll shout it from the rooftops if that's what it takes.

"Blake! You're crazy!" She pulled me into a soft kiss.

"Hello? Is anybody there?" A voice echoed outside the cottage window.

"Shit! Who's that?" Lily bounced out of bed, pulling up her denim shorts and tossing me my pants.

I shrugged. "Probably the agent." I legged into my pants and zipped up the fly as she pulled on her Ramones T-shirt she wore yesterday.

"The agent? Why?" I laughed at the sight of her. Gorgeous just-fucked hair and swollen lips. I guess I wasn't much better. "Oh my God, look at us. We're so flippin' obvious." She raked her hands through her hair in an attempt to neaten it.

"I don't care." I laughed, grabbing her hand, our fingers intertwining as we walked outside.

"Roger will care when he knows we've been sleeping in his styled furniture!"

"I'll buy it off him."

We stepped outside, and Roger stood at the door looking between us.

"Blake? And Lily, what are you doing here?"

"Oh ah..." she mumbled something even I couldn't understand.

"Like I said on the phone, Roger. We're not selling."

Lily looked up at me, a huge grin appearing on her face.

"What do you mean? A lovely couple from the city has

offered well over the asking price. Lily's signed the papers already."

A look of alarm flashed across Lily's face. "Only because I thought Blake had signed."

"Well, I haven't, and I won't." I tossed her a reassuring smile.

Roger threw his hands in the air in a moment of unprofessionalism. Hell, I probably would have done the same too, if my client had dicked me around.

It only took a minute to calm Roger down, especially since I told him I'd buy all the furniture from him and still pay his commission. He walked along the pathway shutting the gate behind him.

"Why didn't you sign?" Lily asked me after he'd left.

Leading her toward the orchard with our hands still interlaced, I sat under the pear tree, and she sat beside me. "Because this place is special. You have made it so. It's our home now, you and me, beautiful. And this is the start of forever."

THE END

EPILOGUE

"Tonight is about you, Jazzie. Lil and I are celebrating having you back in Seaview. I'm already missing you, knowing you're leaving us again so soon."

"And we are celebrating Lily and Blake!" Jazzie added, placing her hand atop Lily's. "I can't tell you how happy I am to see you guys are together. You are honestly so perfect for each other."

"Aww, thanks, honey. I'd have to agree with you there." Lily split into a warm smile.

"Excuse me, ladies, these are for you." The waiter held a tray with three glasses of champagne.

"We didn't order any champagne," Lily said.

The waiter turned his attention from Lily to me. "Courtesy of the gentleman at the bar for you, miss," he said, tilting his head in the direction of the bar behind him.

Me? Without waiting for a response, he placed a flute filled with pale yellow bubbles in front of me, then gave the remaining glasses to the girls.

"Thank you." I craned my neck to peer past the lanky waiter toward the bar.

Overhanging vines and wrought iron candelabras hung from the ceiling. I cast my gaze below. There, a mysterious man with dark-brown locks, tanned skin, and a body fit for an Ironman Challenge stared back at me. Any other night I'd take him home, especially since his burning stare took me to another hemisphere, but not tonight. Tonight wasn't about me.

Jazzie turned around and whisper-mouthed. "Who is that?"

"I don't know. But it doesn't matter. I'm with my girls." When I was out with my girls, I gave them my full attention. With Jazzie living in New York with Kit and Lily and Blake joining firmly at the hip, it was rare for the three of us to get together these days. So tonight, no man, no matter how blisteringly handsome, was going to get in the way.

The waiter smiled before retreating.

"Holy hell. Who *is* that?" Lily said, twisting her neck.

Again, as if on its own accord, my gaze shifted to him. Our eyes collided, and his lips tipped into a lopsided grin. I held up my glass and gave him a nod of appreciation for our drinks while trying to ignore the fizzle shooting up my spine.

The Adonis would have to be put on ice...

Forcing myself to look away once again, I returned my attention back to my girls, but Jazzie's stare remained on him.

"Oh, he's coming over." Jazzie whipped her head back around, her eyes as wide as the half-eaten cronuts in front of us. "Damn, girl, he is handsome." A giggle rolled her off her back.

Thundering palpitations knocked at my chest with each step he drew closer to our table. He sauntered across the busy restaurant floor, his almond-shaped eyes glued to mine.

"Good evening, ladies," he said with a wide smile. His voice, rich like mahogany, was almost as tempting as his scent of cinnamon and cedarwood invading my nostrils. Dark, well-kept stubble adorned his square jaw, and catlike green-blue eyes sidelined me more than I'd like to admit.

"Hi!" Jazzie and Lily said in unison like the choir from *Sister Act.*

Smiling, he returned his focus to me.

He had the kind of hair you'd love to run your hands through, long on top with tapered sides. I swallowed. *How long has it been?*

"Thanks for the drinks, but as you can see, we're having a girls' night."

"I can see that," he said, his cemented stance unshakable.

I tilted my chin. "So, that means no men."

"Is that a rule you have?" he asked.

"Rule?" Lily interjected. "Amber loves her rules."

Damn, Lil, would you just shut it.

"Amber." His glare, prey-like and unmoving, sent pulses between my thighs.

Raising an eyebrow, I questioned, "Can you take a hint, Casanova, or are you as arrogant as your good looks?"

Lily laughed, and Jazzie covered her mouth, but he didn't show any reaction. He stood, unperturbed. Dressed in casual jeans and a crisp baby-blue shirt with the sleeves rolled up, you'd be mistaken to think he fit in if it wasn't for his expensive tan loafers.

I crossed my legs under the table. His arrogance wasn't like the other twenty-somethings who tried it on. Where others would have scampered, he stayed, unfazed by my rebuttal, like he knew he would win, as if he always got what he wanted.

My skin hummed from my neck down. *No, not tonight.*

"I'll be at the bar when you change your mind." He smiled, and at this distance, it revealed a set of movie-star teeth.

"And they say whales have enormous balls!" Lily licked the macaroon crumb that dotted her mouth.

"Ah, Mr. Full of Himself is pretty damn gorgeous, though. Right, Amber?" Jazzie asked.

"Sure, he is. And any other night, I'd probably take him home and lose myself in him, but—"

"And then what? Don't get his number because of your rules?"

"You know my rules keep me safe. What I was going to say before you cut me off, but I won't, because how often do I get to see you both now? Our weekly dinners have been non-existent since you moved to New York, Jazzie." I took another bite of the cronut. Damn, it was good.

"And, Lily, you and Blake are inseparable."

She looked at me all dreamy with wedding bells in her eyes. "We truly are."

I bit the side of my cheek, my gaze diverting to the mystery man at the bar.

There were certainly no wedding bells in my eyes.

WANT MORE?

Want more of Blake and Lily…Click on the link below for the extended epilogue…

https://dl.bookfunnel.com/hpjkxgsa4r

ALSO BY MISSY WALKER

ELITE MEN OF MANHATTAN SERIES

Forbidden Lust

Forbidden Love

Lost Love

Missing Love

SMALL TOWN DESIRES

Trusting the Rockstar

Trusting the Ex

Trusting the Player

Join Missy's Club

Hear about exclusive book releases, teasers and box sets before anyone else.

Sign up to her newsletter here:
www.authormissywalker.com

Become part of Missy's Facebook Crew
www.facebook.com/AuthorMissyWalker

ACKNOWLEDGMENTS

This one was tough. I lost my young father to cancer in the midst of writing this. And the fact that I'd already plotted Alistair's death before Dad's passing was somewhat eerie.

To anyone who has lost someone dearest to them, I acknowledge you.

Thanks to all who helped me put this book out, just in time! Gabby, my editor, thank you. William P, your intimate knowledge of everything hedge fund related helped shape Blake's character, so cheers.

Mum, my number one fan. Thanks for reading and rereading again! I'll try to put more Bj's in the next book! *OMG… yes, she said that*!

Bev. Without you, I honestly couldn't have gone through this year. You put the colour in my rainbow. Even on the cloudiest, coldest of days, you shine bright.

Since my debut novel, Trusting a Rockstar, I've received amazing support from fellow readers, authors and bookstagrammers which has—to be completely honest—blown me away.

You never know if your writing resonates with readers, or

if it will become words on a page eroded with time. All I know is I love writing. I love the escape writing brings and if it brings a tiny slither or a whopping slice of escapism and joy in your life; it makes me abundantly happy too.

If you would like to leave a review, I would be forever grateful. Reviews can really help a new author stand out from the thousands of other Amazon authors out there, especially in the romance genre.

I'm so humbled you've taken a chance on a new author and I can't wait to bring you more.

Cheers,

Missy x

ABOUT THE AUTHOR

Missy is an Australian author who writes kissing books with equal parts angst and steam. Stories about billionaires, forbidden romance, and second chances roll around in her mind probably more than they ought to.

When she's not writing, she's taking care of her two daughters and doting husband and conjuring up her next saucy plot.

Inspired by the acreage she lives on, Missy regularly distracts herself by visiting her orchard, baking naughty but delicious foods, and socialising with her girl squad.

Then there's her overweight cat Charlie, chickens, rabbit and bees if she needed another excuse to pass the time.

If you like Missy Walker's books, consider leaving a review and following her here:

tiktok.com/@authormissywalker
instagram.com/missywalkerauthor
facebook.com/AuthorMissyWalker
www.amazon.com/Missy-Walker
bookbub.com/profile/missy-walker

Printed in Great Britain
by Amazon